## *There was a whirl of movement.*

And before her scream could find voice, a hand clamped over her lips. Flailing with her fists, she struggled to free herself.

"Kathy."

Her name was spoken in a hoarse whisper; then she was dragged against a rock-solid chest. She thrust her knee forward in absolute terror and heard a soft grunt. He released her, but before she could escape, his arms were around her again, dragging her back to him.

"Kathy! For the love of God, it's me!"

She froze. Hysteria rose within her. She had conjured him from the illusions of her mind. She had thought about him, and now he was there.

Brent wasn't dead at all. He was with her, and he was real.

Dear Reader,

This month we're bringing you an absolutely stellar lineup of books. In fact, I hardly know where to begin. First up is *Runaway*, by Emilie Richards. She delivers exactly the kind of knockout emotional punch she's come to be known for. This is the first of two novels about sisters separated by deception and distance, and it's a book with a very different sort of subject: teen runaways, the dangers they face and the lengths they sometimes have to go in order to survive. Next month's *The Way Back Home* completes the circle. I truly believe these two books will live in your memory for a long, long time.

Theresa Weir has written for Silhouette Romance until now, and has also tried her hand at mainstream romance adventure. In *Iguana Bay* she makes her debut appearance in Silhouette Intimate Moments, and what a stunner this book is! The hero is anything but ordinary, as you'll discover the minute you meet him, and his meeting with the heroine is no less noteworthy. And lest you think that's all we have in store, the month is rounded out by two veterans of the bestseller lists and the award rosters: Heather Graham Pozzessere and Marilyn Pappano.

Later in the year, the excitement will continue with new books from favorites such as Linda Howard, Kathleen Korbel and Linda Shaw, to name only a few. The moments are never dull at Silhouette Intimate Moments, so join us for all of them.

Yours,

Leslie J. Wainger
Senior Editor and Editorial Coordinator

# Forever
# My Love

## HEATHER GRAHAM POZZESSERE

*Silhouette Intimate Moments*

Published by Silhouette Books New York

**America's Publisher of Contemporary Romance**

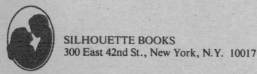

**SILHOUETTE BOOKS**
300 East 42nd St., New York, N.Y. 10017

Copyright © 1990 by Heather Graham Pozzessere

ISBN: 0-373-07340-2

First Silhouette Books printing June 1990

Printed in the U.S.A.

## *HEATHER GRAHAM POZZESSERE*

considers herself lucky to live in Florida, where she can indulge her love of water sports, like swimming and boating, year-round. Her background includes stints as a model, actress and a bartender. She was once actually tied to the railroad tracks to garner publicity for the dinner theater where she was acting. Now she's a full-time wife, mother of four and, of course, a writer of historical and contemporary romances.

Dedicated with thanks and very best wishes to
Dr. Lars Jensen, Dr. Virginia Carver
and Sharon Kifkinif,
for managing to make me laugh
when I was very, very nervous.

And to Rhonda Glicksberg,
for being so very sweet and kind,
and helping to make this baby
such a warm and wonderful experience.

# Chapter 1

Kathy heard the music long before Shanna called her to the living room to watch the television. And despite the years, the pain and the endless things that had gone wrong, she felt the poignant tug on her heart that she always felt whenever she saw Brent, heard a piece of his music, saw his picture in a newspaper or heard the husky whisper of his voice.

"Mother! Come out and see Dad!"

Kathy gritted her teeth and smoothed out the comforter she had just tossed over her bed. Don't growl, smile, she warned herself. If there had been one decent thing she and Brent had managed to do, it was their raising of Shanna. Neither of them had ever said a negative thing about the other to their daughter.

And now she was almost grown up, a beautiful young woman with white-gold hair, fabulous blue eyes and a figure that was both slim and curved, and entirely enchanting.

It was getting harder and harder to believe that she was no longer a child, Kathy thought. Sometimes she found it amazing that she and Brent had created a child with such startling beauty, and then again, sometimes she smiled wistfully and thought, why not? Had she been so very different herself way back when?

And hadn't Brent been the most gorgeous man she had ever seen when she had first met him?

"Mother!" Shanna called.

For a moment Kathy's fingers curled tightly around the quilted comforter, then she straightened, inhaling, exhaling. She knew Shanna was watching Brent's new video.

He and the other four musicians that formed the Highlanders had just cut a new album. She had read about it in *People*. She knew Johnny Blondell fairly well, and had never been especially fond of him. He had a penchant for high living and verbally abusing his wives—she had lost count of how many. Keith Montgomery was originally an Iowa farm boy, and he had never lost the sense of home and old-fashioned values. Kathy was sorry for Keith. He was the one who deserved the breaks, and she had read that his wife had recently been killed in a car accident, leaving him with an infant son. Then there were Larry and Thomas Hicks, brothers famous for their haunting harmonies. Kathy knew them from the old days but knew practically nothing personal about them except that they were both very talented, and as rumor held true, equally temperamental.

The band was quite an array of talent all the way around, Kathy thought. Brent was supposed to be one of the top five guitarists alive, ranking number one at times, depending on the opinion of the reviewer. Johnny was an ace drummer, Keith was extraordinary on keyboards, and the Hicks brothers had their fantastic harmony. The group was destined for success once again.

If only she could distance herself, their new video would probably be wonderfully entertaining to watch.

If only Brent wasn't among the company...

It wouldn't be as bad as watching as the old videos, Kathy assured herself. She wouldn't see the Brent she had fallen in love with—the tall, rangy man with the sensual amber eyes, the rugged face, the dark sandy hair that fell so seductively over one eye.

This was a new video. With any luck, Brent would be half-bald, liver-spotted, bent over and full of warts.

In the doorway she paused with a certain amusement. She'd better hope that he wasn't in that bad a condition. He was only four years her senior, and she didn't want to think that she was rotting away herself. Not quite yet, anyway.

She hurried down the hallway to the large living room. The television was against the wall near the brick fireplace. The floor was laid with Mexican tiles and little studs of old English coats of arms at the angles where four tiles met. Shanna was stretched out on a cow-skin rug that she had dragged to within a few inches of the television set.

"Dad let me watch them filming one day," Shanna said excitedly, aware that her mother had come at last, but not turning her glance from the television. "Of course, it isn't the same at all, because all the images have to be combined. Well, you know!"

Kathy knew. She still knew something about the business, even though they had been divorced for three years.

Three years didn't erase fifteen. She had never realized that more thoroughly than now, standing barefoot, her hands shoved into the pockets of her cutoffs, staring at the television.

He hadn't gone bald. He hadn't changed a bit.

And the video might be a group effort, but this particular song was Brent's. All Brent's. He was the one singing. His distinctive voice carried the melody with a husky hypnotism that was his trademark.

He was seated on a tall stool, his old guitar on his lap, his smile easy and friendly as he strummed the strings or glanced at one of the other musicians. If anything, his shoulders had broadened in acceptance of the fact that he was forty-one now, and she had a sneaky suspicion that his chest was more richly haired. He wore age well, she thought, very well.

He was even more striking than when she had first met him. Some of the years that had gone past were evident in his eyes. They were still full of enigma, but she thought their whiskey-colored depths betrayed a few other emotions—pain, loss, wisdom and acceptance. Did her eyes look like that? she wondered.

"Doesn't he look great, Mother?"

"Yes," Kathy answered evenly. "Yes, he does."

As videos were prone to do, this one changed suddenly. The musicians were no longer in the studio. They were out on a boat, fishing. Brent was in a chair, fighting what must have been a whopper. A young bikini-clad beauty was behind him, laughing delightedly, draping her near-naked body over his naked back.

She had been right, Kathy thought. That chest of his was more richly furred than ever with fine gold-tipped hairs. He was tanned and bronze, and his stomach was still as lean as a whipcord. She felt a tremor somewhere in the pit of her belly and for a moment she intensely hated the blond girl.

It's over between us, Kathy told herself. It had been over for a very long time. Their marriage had fallen apart just like Humpty Dumpty. It had shattered in so many pieces that no one could ever put it together again. And it hadn't been the music business or a blonde or a brunette that had caused the breakup. It had been the big blows of life, followed by the darkness that had suddenly covered them. They hadn't been able to pull together, and so they had fallen apart. Only then had the blondes come into it, and they had both known it. They might have remained friends if they hadn't quarreled quite so passionately at the end.

There had been the last awful fight with its tragic consequences. Afterward he had treated her like a fragile rose, and he had kept his distance. If he had cried, he had never let her see. She knew he had sworn he would never hurt her again, but all that really hurt was that he wouldn't come near her.

Yes, it was over.

Kathy gritted her teeth and managed to put a tight clamp on the emotions that should have passed away with the years. She swallowed the hurt and tried to remind herself that she really wished him well. She wished Brent happiness.

But she still hated the blonde, she decided.

"Marla Harrington. She's a twit!" Shanna said disgustedly.

"You know her?" Kathy curled up on the leather sofa.

Shanna's golden head was nodding. "She's a twit," she repeated.

"A good-looking one," Kathy commented.

"She hangs all over Dad, and he isn't interested."

Kathy doubted that. Brent was looking at the woman, smiling, laughing. Marla Harrington was tall, with short silky hair that moved with her, like the hair in a shampoo commercial. She was lean and lithe, except around the cleavage area. She had a beautiful smile and mahogany eyes. Laughter was touching those eyes, just as it touched Brent's. It was a fun song they were singing, with an easy pop rhythm. Kathy knew already it would be a big hit. The single would probably reach number one immediately. Shanna had told her that the album had several great songs and that she would love it. Kathy believed her daughter, but she didn't want to hear the album.

"What makes you think your dad isn't interested?" Kathy asked idly. She stared at her toes.

Then she had Shanna's attention. Shanna turned from the television to stare at her. "He just isn't. I know it. He hasn't been interested in anyone since you two broke up."

"Oh." Kathy tried to speak lightly. "That isn't true. Give him a chance. He'll find the right woman."

"He's still in love with you. And you're still in love with him."

She breathed deeply. "Shanna," she said very softly. "Children of divorced parents always want to believe that. But it just isn't true. I haven't even seen your father in three years."

"It doesn't matter," Shanna said. She turned to the television. The video had come to an end, and the disc jockey was announcing it as a surefire hit. She went on to introduce the musicians, ending with Brent McQueen. "The master is surely back to it here! Some thought that he'd never really be back after the death of his infant son four years ago, but as you've heard today—"

The television was off. Shanna had leaped to her feet to flick it off. Now she stared at Kathy. "Mother, I'm sorry, I didn't mean—"

"It's all right," Kathy told her. She managed to smile and get to her feet. "It's all right, really, sweetheart. It happened so long ago, and I've still got you." She gave Shanna a fierce, tight hug, and her daughter, warm, protective, giving, hugged her back. Suddenly, there were tears stinging Kathy's eyes. She held tight to her daughter. "Honestly, Shanna, I have you, and you're precious to me, you know that, don't you?"

She pulled away and managed a huge smile. "And you're taller than I am, too, now. That's not quite fair."

Shanna laughed. "Mom, neither of us is exactly an Amazon."

Kathy grinned. It was all right. She had control again. She could push it all into a far corner of her heart, where it belonged. She released Shanna, certain that no matter how good and loving her daughter was it wasn't good to hold too tight. "Aren't you going to be late for that trip of yours?" she asked Shanna.

Shanna glanced at her watch. "Oh! Gosh, I just might be running late. David should be here any minute. Now, Mom, you're really not going to worry, are you? His parents are both wonderful sailors, and you know that I'm a darned good diver and—"

The doorbell rang. Patty McGiver, Kathy's secretary and housekeeper, chirped merrily, "I'll get it!"

Patty had a pretty, wholesome face, but she insisted on wearing her steel-gray hair in an old-fashioned bun on top of her head. She had the look of a resolute old maid, and though Kathy wondered why Patty had never wanted a family of her own, she was too grateful to have the woman to ponder the question often.

Kathy went by her maiden name, O'Hara, and she lived in an old, quiet section of Coconut Grove, Florida, where her neighbors were discreet and respected their privacy. She had her own business, an advertising firm, and needed the help at home. She

liked the house, and she even liked cleaning—it
helped her think—but there just weren't enough
hours in the day for everything. Patty was a god-
send.

"Hello, there, young man!" Patty greeted David
Brennan.

"Mom, now—" Shanna began.

"I'm not worried. I know the Brennans are ex-
ceptional sailors, and I trust you and David." She
had been an overprotective parent for a long time.
She hadn't been able to help it. Now she was trying
very hard to let loose a little. If she didn't, she knew
she would smother her child. And Shanna was an
angel. She'd seen enough of some of the music crowd
to stay away from drugs. A senior in high school, she
got excellent grades, and she seemed to love her
mother and father equally. She lived with Kathy, but
she spent every other weekend with her father, and
shared her holidays carefully.

Brent had always been there for Shanna, Kathy
thought. No matter what he had been doing, he had
never failed his daughter. She would have to say that
for him.

There was much more to be said for Brent, she
knew. She also knew she was still in love with him,
that she always would be.

But life went on. She had learned that the hard
way.

"Honest, I'm not worried," Kathy reassured Shanna. She walked with her daughter to the doorway where David, six feet two, blond, all-American with a wide grin, was waiting.

"Hi, Mrs. McQueen." David never had comprehended why she chose to use her maiden name. "Please don't worry—"

"I'm not worried," Kathy vowed again.

Shanna laughed, stood on tiptoe and gave David a kiss on the cheek. "She's already been through it, Dave. I'll just get my things."

"You're going out from Key Largo, right?" Kathy asked as Shanna ran to her room.

"Right. We can be reached by radio, you know," David assured her. "And you are still invited."

Kathy shook her head. "Thanks, David. I'm having dinner with Axel Fisher."

Shanna had appeared with a duffel bag. "Of Axel Fisher Skin Care Products," she said sweetly. Shanna didn't like Axel. He was tall, urbane, and attractive, but he knew very little about dealing with young people. He was attractive in a very studied way, like the male models who showed off his products. He was tanned, his hair was styled, not just cut, and he carefully allotted so many hours of the week to his health club.

He was nice, though. Attentive and caring. Kathy wondered if she would find fault with any man, and if Shanna would do the same. Shanna had found

fault with Marla Harrington on her mother's behalf, and she found fault with Axel on her father's
behalf.

"You could have brought along Mr. Fisher—"
David began.

"No, she could not!" Shanna said emphatically.
Then she flushed and apologized. "Sorry, Mom, it's
just—"

"That's okay!" Kathy laughed. "Go out with
your father and the twit, but draw the line on me."

"Oh, Mom."

"I'm teasing, I swear it. Now go on, and have a
great time. And David, give your parents my re-
gards, and my thanks for the invitation. See you
Monday sometime."

"Bye, Mom, bye, Patty." Shanna gave Patty a
quick kiss on the cheek, then hugged her mother
fiercely. David solemnly shook her hand then told
Patty goodbye. Patty and Kathy stood together
waving as the two went down the walk and out the
high gate that surrounded the property.

"You should turn on the security system now,"
Patty told her.

Kathy shrugged. She didn't worry much about security. There was a gate house at the front of the ex-
clusive housing estate, and the entire area was off the
beaten track. They were old houses for Miami, built
in the early twenties, and most of the houses were
still owned by members of the original families. Be-

sides that, Sam, her fiercely loyal Doberman, guarded her house, and only friends could walk by Sam. He knew who belonged at the house and who didn't.

"I'll set the alarm once you head for your sister's, Patty," Kathy told her. "I'm going to have a bath, but I'll be out in time to say goodbye."

"Make sure you set that thing!" Patty warned her, hurrying to her room behind the kitchen. "Alarm can't be any good if you don't bother to set the darn thing. And a high-crime district like this one—"

"The grove has a high crime ratio," Kathy said, smiling. "Not our little neighborhood."

Patty sniffed and disappeared. Kathy walked to her bathroom, determined on a long soak in a bubble bath. Then she realized that the scented salts she had just bought were still in the kitchen cabinet where she had stuck the department store bag to get it out of the way.

She went into the kitchen, found the bath salts and took the glass of wine that Patty insisted she bring with her. When she was ensconced in the big oval tub, she took a long swallow of the wine. It was therapeutic. It warmed her to her toes. It warmed away some of the tension deep within her.

She leaned her head back and closed her eyes. Her heart was thundering. Close your eyes, she told herself. Relax. She had to relax.

But trying to relax made her think more. About the tub, about the house, about Brent.

She'd always loved the tub. She loved the bathroom—it was huge and had been redone before they bought the house from her mother's cousin. There were his and her toilet stalls, a giant marble island with a skylight above and double sinks, a shower stall and the tub. It, too, had a skylight, plus a glass wall beside it. Outside the glass wall were shrubs and flowers and a high redwood privacy fence. The back of the property faced the bay, so a breeze was always touching the shrubs and flowers, moving them gently.

She opened her eyes. The hot steam of the bath rose around her, and she felt her tension begin to ease. She took a long sip of her wine, then closed her eyes and leaned her head against the rim of the tub.

If Brent were still her husband, she could have opened one eye and found him standing there. He seemed to sense when she was going to settle in for a long bath. And he would appear in a terry robe, its V neck displaying his chest, with the mat of sandy and gold hair and taut muscles and the pulse at the base of his throat. He'd show up with a lazy, wicked gleam in his eyes and say her name so softly that it would seem to come off the breeze. She'd smile, and before she'd know it he was stepping in with her, heedless of his robe, which would be soaked and floating around them. He'd hand her a glass of wine and pull her into his arms. Then he would ask her huskily, "Isn't it fun to have a little money at last? It can't buy happiness, but hey, it did buy one hell of a bathtub, huh?"

She would laugh, and he would kiss her, and their legs would tangle together. She always thought it had to be hard for him to get comfortable. She was a mere five foot three, whereas Brent was six foot two or more, but he would tell her it was impossible to be uncomfortable with her in his arms.

They would laugh and remember what their first place had been like. She had been eighteen and he had been twenty-two and they were trying to live off his club-date fees while she went to school and worked part-time at the Burger Barn. She had been desperately in love with him right from the very first time she had seen him playing his guitar at a friend's wedding. He had been so tall, lean, fascinating with his deep, penetrating eyes that seemed to gaze upon her with ancient wisdom, to sparkle with laughter, to deepen with something more intense. He had appeared older than his years, or maybe it was just that he had already been through so much—a wretched childhood as an orphan, three years in the service, a third of that time in the volatile Middle East, then attendance at a college and survival with his music at the same time.

Kathy had been a senior in high school, and from the first time his eyes had met hers across the room with neon strobes bouncing and gliding, she had been in love. Later, when the band had stopped playing and records had filled the break time, he had walked straight to her, and he had danced with her. She had stared into his eyes and slowly smiled. When he had gone to play again, he sang a song he had written, a soft, romantic ballad he called "Forever My Love." She had felt his voice touch her. It was husky, sure, a tenor with just the slightest hint of a masculine rasp. His eyes had been on her, and she knew that the song had been sung just for her. He admitted later that he'd never sung it in public before, that it had never come together before, but when he had met her, the words, the music, everything had just fallen in place.

Forever, my love...

Well, they had tried it, they had vowed it, and maybe a certain amount of the love would always be there. But on that night so long ago when they had first danced they hadn't known all that was to come between them, the good times and the bad, the heaven and the hell. Nor had they had any way to see the pain that was to befall them.

Kathy sighed softly, opening her eyes. Darkness was falling rapidly. She looked up and saw a murky sky with the stars just beginning to dot the gray.

She started suddenly, thinking that something had tapped against the redwood privacy screen. Sam, she decided. It had to have been Sam. Still, she straightened and stared out. All she saw was the darkness. She rose out of the tub, passing the gilt-edged Victorian mirror by the closet. She paused and smoothed a stray strand of hair. She was still staring at herself seconds later, she realized. Looking for age lines? she taunted silently. Standing away from the mirror, she saw that she did resemble her daughter a great deal. They had the same huge blue eyes and the same soft blond hair, which they wore layered just past their shoulders. And they were both lean and petite with moderate but ample curves, as she liked to call them.

It was when she stepped closer to the mirror that the differences became obvious. Shanna lacked the tiny lines and grooves around the eyes that defined Kathy's age. Maybe it was more than the lines. Maybe it was something in her eyes that betrayed her so quickly. Maybe she needed something to clear them away...

"No," she told the mirror. "Those are character lines, and I earned every single one of them." Managing a rueful smile, she told herself she was not going to wax nostalgic any longer.

She started down the hallway and across the living room. It was only when she was halfway to the kitchen that she realized the television was on and that Patty was standing stock-still in the middle of the room, staring at the screen.

"—and it is believed at this time that Brent Mc-
Queen was also aboard the yacht *Theodosia* when it
exploded. McQueen and Johnny Blondell were re-
portedly having serious problems, and McQueen was
expected to lay his grievances before Blondell. The
body of Johnny Blondell has been found, but not
McQueen's. The search team will have to wait for the
fire on board to die down before they can look for
the remains of any further victims. No one knows the
cause of the explosion at this time, but arson is
expected."

Kathy inhaled sharply, unable to comprehend
what she was hearing. She walked closer to the television. The anchorman was still talking. A picture of
Brent was flashed across the screen, a picture almost
twenty years old, one with her in it. His arm was
protectively around her, there were conspiratorial
smiles on both of their faces, and they were both very
beautiful in the simple happiness that radiated from
their faces. The picture had been taken at the air-
port, right after their marriage.

Her hands clenched into fists at her side and she
fell to her knees, a ragged, anguished cry wrenched
from her lips. Patty walked to her and patted her
shoulders. "Kathy, they don't know anything yet. He
probably wasn't aboard the yacht. You can't jump to
conclusions like those stupid newsmen."

Kathy looked from the screen to Patty, dazed.

"He was having problems with Johnny and he might have died because of them. That little rat! Johnny Blondell was a junky, a womanizer, a slime and an abuser—"

"Kathy, the man is dead."

"And he might have taken Brent with him! Oh, my God!" Kathy breathed. "Shanna! Thank God she can't have heard anything yet!" She hopped to her feet, raced to the phone and tried to call the television station to find out more information. When she finally got through, they were vague, saying that the police didn't know anymore yet. "Watch at eleven, and we'll bring you up-to-date information," a deep male voice told her.

"Wait a minute! You're reporting very irresponsibly!" Kathy swore. "You're saying a man might be dead—"

"Honey, wait till eleven. What does all this matter anyway?"

"It's going to matter tremendously to his daughter, in whose name I intend to sue you!" Kathy said, and slammed down the receiver.

"Kathy—" Patty began sympathetically.

"I'm all right!"

She wasn't all right. She was ready to burst into tears. She was torn apart for Shanna. And she was bleeding herself.

A bell clanged, warning them that someone was at the gate. Kathy frowned and hurried to the door,

looking through the peephole that showed whoever
was on the porch and also magnified the scene at the
gate.

A man was standing there.

"My God!" she whispered. "It's about Brent, I
know it!"

"Kathy," Patty began again. "Wait—"

Kathy threw open the door and hurried down the
porch steps and along the flower-bordered tile path.
The dog barked, and Kathy told him to get back. She
swung open the gate and cried out when she saw that
it wasn't just a man, but Robert McGregor, a plain-
clothes cop who had gone to school with her and
been a friend to both her and Brent.

Fear rushed through her. He had come to tell her
that Brent was dead. The world spun, and she
thought she was going to crash to the ground.

"Kathy! It's all right. Listen to me, please. I
haven't got much time, I've got to get back to the
marina. Listen, he's not dead, I'm sure he's not. I
talked to Brent tonight."

"What?" she gasped and sagged against him. He
caught her.

"Let me get you back to the house."

"No, no. Tell me now. Talk to me, Robert,
please."

"Brent called me. He wanted to talk with me
about something. He said he wanted to see me before he saw Johnny. So I know he's all right."

"But you haven't . . . you haven't seen him?" she whispered.

He shook his head. "But I saw the newscast, and I knew you must be going insane. Now listen to me. I'll find Brent."

She nodded stiffly. "I'll go with you."

"No. You'll go into the house and you'll calm down and relax. *I'll* find Brent."

"But—"

"Please, Kathy. Come on now, I'll take you in."

She straightened and offered him a tight smile. "No, I'm fine, I promise. Go on. And thank you! Bless you!" she added in a whisper as she watched him go down the walk. Then she hurried into the kitchen. "It was Robert McGregor," she told Patty. "He says that Brent wasn't on the yacht. He talked to Brent."

Patty nodded. "Why don't you lie down for a few minutes?"

"If you promise to listen for the door or the phone."

Patty smiled her agreement, and Kathy headed for her bedroom. She was numb. She had to believe Brent was all right. She had to.

She entered her room and closed the door behind her. She had never changed the room. There was the huge closet, the entertainment center, the stereo, the bookcases, the television and video machine. The woodwork had been carved to complement the turn-of-the-century dresser set. Old and new, masculine and feminine touches, were combined. It was a room designed for a couple to share. A place to laugh and dream together, to hide away from an intrusive world.

She covered her face with her hands.

The room almost looked as if she had been waiting for Brent to return for the past three years. But now it seemed he never ever would.

Nonsense. Robert had said that Brent was all right.

She was too jittery to sleep. Knowing only another bath would calm her down, she hurried into the bathroom, trying to function normally. After turning on the tap, adding more bubble bath, she pulled the drape on the window of the door that led out to the pool and cabana, and mechanically stripped off her clothing in the bedroom. She stepped into the water.

There was a whirl of darkness in the shadows of the night, and before her scream could find voice, a hand clamped hard over her lips. She threw up a spray of water, flailing with her fists to free herself.

"Kathy!"

She heard her name in a hoarse whisper and still she struggled desperately. When she was dragged against a rock-hard chest, she thrust her knee forward in terror and heard a soft grunt.

She managed to escape the arms, but before she could step from the tub the arms were around her again, dragging her back. She opened her mouth to scream but her assailant's arms and hands were on her mouth once again. He was holding her in a vise-like grip. She writhed and twisted to no avail, panicking when she felt fingers just beneath her breast.

"Kathy! Kathy! For the love of God, it's me!"

She froze. Hysteria rose within her. She had conjured him from the illusions of her mind. She had thought about him stepping into the tub with her....

And now he was there.

He wasn't dead at all. He was there, in her bathtub.

He eased his hold. She drew quickly away from him, gathering bubbles around her, staring at him incredulously.

He was real. A lock of dark, damp hair had fallen seductively over his forehead. His eyes were the same deep rich amber, the lines around them a bit deeper, but attractive. He had a handsome face with a fine bone structure that indicated integrity. The face had aged remarkably well, and it was even more fascinating now for all that character etched into it. She stared at him and knew his death would have killed her deep inside, and that life would have lost all meaning for her. She was still in love with him, and she always had been.

"Brent!"

"Kathy." His voice was husky and low. It was sexy and sensual and deeply masculine, and it touched her as it had always touched her. "Kathy, shut up, please. I need your help."

"Why did you attack me?"

"Why did you scream?"

"I always scream when strange men enter my bathroom."

He grinned. "I'm not a strange man."

"Oh, I do beg to differ!" she retorted. "You're an extremely strange man!"

"Kathy—"

"Brent, for the love of God, would you please get out of the bathtub?"

His smile remained in place. "Brings back memories, doesn't it?"

"Out!"

"Kathy, I need your help."

"Get out of my tub!"

He rose and stood dripping on the bath rug. He pulled off his sneakers and socks. "I hope there's still something of mine around here somewhere," he muttered, unbuttoning his shirt.

"What are you doing?" she nearly shrieked. His sodden shirt fell to the floor. He was half naked, his jeans clinging tightly to the line of his hard, lean thighs and the muscled curve of his buttocks. The bronze chest that she had ached to touch was suddenly before her, and she was so unnerved she could scarcely bear it.

She leaped up, heedless of her nudity, grabbed a bath towel and wrapped it around herself. But her fingers were trembling and she dropped the towel. He reached for it and handed it to her. Her eyes met his. Then all the emotions that had surged through her in the past few minutes exploded to the surface.

"Damn you! Damn you! You need my help? You broke into my house, you attacked me in the tub—"

"Kathy, *our* house, I still own part of it, remember?"

He was smiling. He was actually smiling. Of course. She was standing there with the towel between them, swearing away, stark naked. Slowly, his lips curled in the way that was so Brent McQueen, and he gave her an easy sensual smile like the one he had given the young woman in the video.

She snatched the towel, then slammed the palms of her hands hard against his chest.

"Kathy—"

"Brent McQueen, how could—"

She broke off as a voice from outside the bedroom door interrupted them. "Kathy!" It was Patty. "Kathy, if you need me..."

For the third time Brent slapped his hand over her mouth. "Tell her you're fine!" he warned her. She stared at him, her eyes narrowing. He was tense and deadly serious. There was something very hard and lethal about him, and despite herself, she shivered.

What in hell was going on?

He had always been hard; the service had done that to him. And he had always been smart, so he had sometimes been cynical. And he had always been more than a bit of a chauvinist, demanding, autocratic.

But this was something new.

"Kathy?" Patty's anxious voice sounded again.

His eyes glittered, dancing in the false light of the room. "Kathy, so help me God!" he said. His hand rose carefully from her mouth, but he still held both her arms in the vise of his fingers.

"Patty wouldn't hurt you!" she whispered.

"Tell her to go away!" Brent insisted in a soft growl.

"You know you don't live here anymore and we're not married anymore and I'm not at your beck and call—"

"Kathy!" He towered over her, his features taut and strained. "Tell her you're fine. Tell her to go away!"

"I can't—"

"You will!"

She stared at him a moment longer, thinking that she ought to tear every hair out of his head. Then he would be bald. And maybe he wouldn't be so attractive.

No, every hair could be out of his head, he could be painted purple and he would still have the raw, masculine charisma that so easily attracted the adoration of women and the admiration of men.

She breathed deeply, then called out softly. "Patty? I'm fine, just getting dressed. I'll be out in a minute."

"Oh! Thank goodness. I heard some noise. I was getting so worried."

Staring at Brent, she listened to Patty's soft footsteps on the carpet as the woman moved away. "So you are alive," she whispered to Brent.

"Disappointed?" he asked her.

"Of course not. Shanna would have been terribly hurt if you had died."

"Just Shanna?" His hands were on her, still holding her close.

"Well, of course, your death would upset me, too. For old time's sake." Once again, she shoved her fists hard against his chest. "Let me go, Brent, and for God's sake, tell me what the hell is going on!"

He didn't let her go, not right away. He caught her hands, and his fingers wound around her wrists. Then he stared at her for what seemed like eons. His eyes flashed gold and fire as they moved over her face, then her form. For a moment, she thought he was going to kiss her. That his lips would touch hers with their special, intimate seal, and all the hurt and pain would be gone, erased, like magic.

There was no such thing as magic, and nothing could erase the things that had gone between them.

He released her and walked out of the bathroom. She followed him, grasped her robe from the bed and quickly slipped into it. Her towel fell to the floor and she realized she could not stand. She sat at the foot of the bed.

He paced, rubbing his temple with his thumb and forefinger.

"Brent?"

He didn't seem to hear her, and only continued to walk across the room.

"Brent?" she repeated. "I've played it your way. Now I asked you to tell me—"

"Dammit, Kathryn, I don't know what is going on."

"But you're alive and—"

"Yes, yes! And I'm alive because I wasn't on that boat. But Johnny's murderer is after me, and I can't quite figure out what the hell is going on." He had stopped pacing and stood before her tensely. Then he dropped to one knee and caught her hands. "You're going to listen to me, Kathryn, and do what I say."

"Brent—"

"You don't owe me anything. But you're going to do what I tell you now!"

It was an order, not an appeal. He really hadn't changed at all.

She pulled her hands away and curled her feet beneath her. "Am I really? Tell me, McQueen, just what it is you're assuming I'm going to do."

## Chapter 2

This really wasn't going at all well, Brent thought, staring at Kathy as she stared at him. He hadn't expected to find her in the bathroom, and he hadn't expected her to scream at the sight of him. Well, all right, so maybe he hadn't expected her to jump up and down with joy, but he hadn't thought it would get so damned physical.

Or that it would hurt so much. As if his heart was being torn out all over again.

He stiffened his spine and squared his shoulders. This had to do with life and death, and she was going to have to listen to him. She had to quit with that imperious stare. But then that was part of Kathy's charisma. She looked like a snow princess with her startling blue, almost cobalt, eyes and silky blond hair. Her features were near perfect. Her face was oval, her cheekbones defined, her lips generous but beautifully shaped, and her eyebrows with a little arch that could give her a look of annoying superiority. Despite that, there had been times when his need to protect her had been enormous. And it could be just like trying to protect a barracuda at times, he reminded himself.

She was still staring at him, waiting.

"Kathy, where is Shanna?" he asked.

She seemed startled. "Out with her boyfriend," she replied. "I get the first questions, Brent. Why the bathroom? After three years apart, most men would have rung a doorbell."

And after three years, most men might have found a new life, he thought bitterly. He never had. No matter where he went, or what he did, images of Kathy were always there. She intruded on a dance floor, she intruded in bed. Sometimes, alone at night, he'd stare at the ceiling and try to remind himself that they'd had an uncanny ability to fight like warring politicians. But the memories would keep going, and he'd remember the way the fights would end, how they would both be so alive and on fire with passion. And that made the love and tenderness that followed so much sweeter....

But in the end, the pain had just been too much. When he couldn't bear it any longer, he had walked away.

She could have had the decency to change, though, he thought. She hadn't, not a whit. She should have gone gray, or gained fifty pounds, sagged somewhat with the gravity of time. But she hadn't. That was one fact he was sure of from their encounter in the bathtub. She was browned from the sun, slim and still beautifully curved. Her eyes were enormous and exquisitely blue. Her blond hair was soft and curled over her shoulders, looking sleek and achingly inviting.

"Kathy," he said wearily, "you're not getting the drift of this—"

"Because you're not telling me anything!" she flared.

He swore softly and turned from her, padding to the closet. With any luck, she wouldn't have burned every single thing he used to own.

"Brent, you're dripping all over the place!" she called irritably after him. "All over my rug—"

He poked his head out of the closet door. "My rug, too," he reminded her pleasantly.

She was on her feet, hands on hips, staring at him. "We agreed to keep the house together until Shanna was twenty-one. I'm to live in it, and we both have the option to buy the other out, or share in the profits if we sell it to someone else. The agreement does not mean that you can enter via the bathroom at any time and soak the place! You're walking all over with those drenched pants."

She knew the second the words were out that she shouldn't have spoken. He stared at her hard, smiled slowly, then unzipped his pants. She turned with a soft oath on her lips because she knew damned well that he was going to strip his pants right off and throw them on the floor.

He did. She heard them fall. "Happy?" he asked her softly.

She strode quickly to the dresser that had always been his, and hunched down to reach the bottom drawer. She found a pair of his briefs, socks and jeans and threw them in the general area of where he was standing.

"Fifteen years and you suddenly want modesty?" he queried in the same soft tone.

"Fifteen, and then three!" she reminded him, her back to him as she fished through her own dresser for jeans and a soft blue knit pullover. She could sense that he hadn't picked up his clothing.

"Am I disturbing you?" he asked, and despite the circumstances, she could hear the humor in his voice.

She turned and looked him straight in the eye. "No." Her gaze started to slip down his body. She couldn't stand there much longer. "Excuse me, I'll take the bathroom. If you think you can refrain from entering it for a few moments, that is?"

His smile slowly deepened. "Well, I'll try, Ms. O'Hara. I'll certainly try."

She headed into the bathroom. She brushed her hair before the mirror over the sink and realized that her hands were shaking badly. She gripped the sink hard to make them stop. *He was alive.* The thought filled her completely. But he was talking in riddles, and she wasn't getting anywhere with him. The past kept leaping before them.

And desire, she reminded herself ruefully. She felt as if she hurt all over and she closed her eyes, wishing desperately that she had fallen out of love, not just out of marriage.

She took a deep breath, swung around and went into the bedroom. Being clothed was much better. Brent was in the closet, but his wet jeans were hanging on the bathroom doorknob. His dry jeans and briefs had disappeared.

He appeared in the doorway a second later, buttoning a tailored striped shirt. "You kept things," he said bluntly.

She shrugged and sat on the bed. "I meant to have you pick them up, or else send them to you. Then I decided you probably didn't need them anymore. So I was going to have them all sent to the refugee camps, but I never did. Brent, tell me what—"

"Exactly where is Shanna?" he demanded, interrupting her.

"She's out with David. I think you know him."

"Where?" he snapped.

"You should have stayed in the army! You would have made a wonderful drill sergeant."

He strode across the room and leaned over her, bracing his hands on the bed. "I need to know where she is," he said tensely.

Before she could reply, there was a tap on the door. "Kathy? Are you all right? I'm not going to leave you alone tonight, you know that," Patty called to her worriedly through the door.

Brent backed away. "She's not going to leave you alone tonight?" he whispered in dismay.

"We thought you were dead, remember?" she whispered.

A smile crooked his lips. "And you were that upset?"

"I couldn't begin to imagine having to tell Shanna," she retorted.

"Kathy, please! Are you all right in there?"

"Why can't I tell Patty?"

He shook his head vehemently. "Tell her to go home. Or to her sister's, or the movies, I don't care where."

With an exaggerated sigh she hurried to the door while Brent flattened himself against the wall. She opened the door. "Patty, please, go on. I know that Brent is all right, and I'm fine. I might even take the boat out to join Shanna just in case she hears something. You go on now."

"But Kathy," Patty protested. "I couldn't leave you alone, not when you were so hysterical."

"But I'm not hysterical now," Kathy insisted, gritting her teeth. "Please, Patty, I'll be fine."

"Well, all right then, but you know where to reach me if you need me," Patty said at last.

"Of course." Kathy gave her a warm hug and a kiss on the cheek.

"And you come out and put on that security system, do you hear me?" Patty charged her.

"Yes," Kathy said dryly. "Yes, I think I should." She followed Patty into the living room. Let Brent pace and fume for a few minutes. He was darned lucky she hadn't set it before. Sam was still the best security in the world, she thought, except that Sam had always loved Brent and apparently hadn't forgotten that for a single moment. The dog had probably licked Brent's face and hands the entire time Brent was sneaking into the bathroom.

Even dogs were traitors!

Kathy spent ten minutes assuring Patty she was fine, then another ten getting her out the door. She started to set the alarm when Brent's voice suddenly made her jump nearly a foot.

"Who the hell is that coming now?" Brent demanded at her shoulder.

She stood on her toes and looked through the peephole.

Axel was at the gate. Sam didn't like Axel very much, so he had started to bark. Axel, very tan, very tall and looking perfectly urbane in very fashionable clothing, was at the gate, swearing.

The bell rang.

"Who is it?" Brent demanded.

"A friend," Kathy murmured.

"A friend?"

"Okay, a friend with whom I have a date," she said.

Axel was still swearing at the dog, and Brent was swearing at her under his breath.

"Couldn't wait for my body to grow cold, huh?"

"I made the date last week," she answered. "And we've been divorced for three years, Brent."

He wasn't going to argue with her over that. Leaning against the door, he stared at her and charged her, "Get rid of him."

She glared at him. "You know, Brent, I did have plans—"

"Get rid of him, Kathy."

"Don't you talk to me like that and—"

"All right, please get rid of him, Kathy." He didn't wait for an answer, but turned and looked through the peep hole. He smiled at her. "Natty dresser, huh?"

"He dresses quite nicely, actually."

"Yep. Just like dating a Ken doll, eh, Barbie?"

"Speaking of Barbies, where is Miss Harrington? Marla, isn't it? Couldn't you have gone to her for help?"

He didn't blink or betray a single emotion. "She isn't the mother of my daughter," he told her simply. "Kathy, please go do something with Mr. Sunshine. I want to get to Shanna as soon as possible."

Her eyes widened with alarm. "Why? What's wrong? What's going to happen to—"

"Kathy, I'll explain, I promise. But Sam is barking loudly enough to wake the dead, and if you don't answer that door, your, er, friend is going to call the police."

"You're blocking my way," she said.

He stepped quickly aside. Kathy hurried down the walk to the gate. "Down, Sam, down!" she told the dog. But Sam was still jumping at the gate, no longer barking, but whining unhappily. He knew Brent was in the house. He was worse than a mother, Kathy thought.

"Sam, down!"

"Kathy, that dog is getting dangerous," Axel warned her.

"He's supposed to be dangerous. He's a guard dog," she said sweetly as she opened the gate. Axel would have come in, but she slipped out quickly, closing the gate on the dog. Axel was frowning, looking at her casual attire. "I know I said that we didn't need to dress for dinner, but—"

"I can't go, Axel," she said.

"What's the matter?"

"Nothing, really. There's, uh, there's been an accident, and Brent's name has been linked with it and I want to stay here in case Shanna calls."

"Oh!" Startled, Axel looked at her worriedly. "Oh, Kathy, I'm really sorry. Of course, we'll cancel dinner. I'm sure you must be very concerned. I'll stay with you—"

"No!" she said quickly, then instantly regretted her outburst. There were nice things, really nice things, about Axel. His concern for her was one. "Axel, please forgive me. I have a horrible headache. I just want to get some rest and be alone. Please. I appreciate your concern and I am so sorry, it's just—"

"Hey!" He caught her face between his hands and held it tenderly, staring into her eyes. "Kathy, it's all right. I understand. Call me if you need me, if I can do anything, anything at all."

She nodded, feeling horribly guilty. He bent and softly kissed her lips, then urged her toward the gate. "Get on in there now."

"I will."

"Set the alarm."

"I will. Right away."

"Call me!"

"I will."

He nodded and started toward his bloodred Ferrari. "You do have Sam!"

Yes, she did have Sam. And Sam could protect her against anyone. Except the one man she most needed protection from.

She locked the gate and waved at Axel, then hurried to the house. The door opened when she reached it. As soon as she stepped inside, it closed behind her. Brent was leaning against it, watching her with a wicked gleam in his eyes.

"A friend, huh?" he asked.

"Yes."

"What a tender farewell."

"He's a tender sort of guy," she said, waving a hand in the air.

He stepped away from the door, and in a second he was standing before her, looking into her eyes. They might have been kids again, volatile, very passionate and insanely jealous.

"So just how serious is it with you and Ken?"

"Axel. His name is Axel," she said sweetly.

"Well?"

She smiled slowly, enjoying the moment. At least she didn't appear on videos with Axel with her chest bared. Maybe it wasn't quite the same thing, but . . .

"He's a friend. And what is it to you, Mr. McQueen?"

"I'm concerned for your welfare, nothing more, Ms. O'Hara," he told her. But his eyes were on her mouth. He wasn't touching her at all, but she felt the warmth that radiated from him as if it was the glow of a fire enveloping her...

"I just wondered if it was the same," he said.

"The same?"

His head lowered and his mouth caught hold of hers, and waves of sensation, memories and more, flooded throughout her limbs and her torso and rushed wickedly along the length of her spine. His tongue flicked softly over her lips and gained entrance. She should have denied his gentle assault, but she could not. She trembled, wishing it wasn't the same, wishing she wasn't so easy. Wishing that Axel's kiss was something pleasant, not unstirring. Wishing that the mere contact with Brent's mouth didn't cause such an explosion of passion and desire....

He stepped back. If she hadn't caught herself instantly, she would have fallen. Her eyes flew open, and she could still feel his mouth touching hers. He was studying her so intently, and she was afraid she would betray her feelings.

"Well?" he said very softly.

"Well, what?" she demanded.

"Is there a difference?"

"Well, no, you haven't changed."

"But you don't love me any more."

"I did for fifteen years. Perhaps now I don't know, but the thought of your kiss—"

"Or the reality of it," he interjected.

"Hmm. Anyway, it doesn't make me want to throw up or anything," she said sweetly.

He groaned softly, then he laughed, and he pulled her to him. She felt the bulge of muscles in his arms and the hardness of his chest, and she suddenly knew that if he came a single hair closer to her, she would burst into tears and beg him to try to explain to her what had gone wrong.

She wound her fingers around his wrist and stepped back. "Brent, what about Shanna? You broke into my bathroom, you made me send Patty away and break a date and now you have me worried senseless and I still haven't the faintest idea what is going on. Tell me!"

He released her. Still comfortable in the house, he strode across the living room toward the kitchen. He opened the refrigerator and pulled out a beer, casting her a curious gaze at the change in her brand.

"Brent—"

"All right," he said. "I'll start with tonight. I was supposed to have dinner with Johnny on that yacht of his. Johnny wanted to keep the Highlanders going for another album and I didn't want to have anything more to do with him."

Kathy pulled a soda from the refrigerator, sat on one of the kitchen counter bar stools and nodded. Brent and Johnny were entirely different people.

"No, we've got to sail down there and get her ourselves. And we should go now, right now. What have you got in here that we can take to eat?"

She stared at him. She couldn't go off with him alone in the boat—she just couldn't. She had a forty-foot sailboat with a great motor that would get them wherever they wanted to go no matter what the weather, but that wasn't the point.

Once, it had been *their* sailboat. He had been the captain and she the first mate and they had spent hours and hours of their free time sailing her—to the Keys, to the Bahamas, wherever they had time to go. They had spent long, lazy afternoons on the boat, sunning, fishing, snorkeling, diving...

Fighting, and making love.

"Kathy, what's the matter with you? We've got to go! What can we pack—"

"We don't need to pack anything."

"What?"

"The—the galley is stocked."

He seemed to freeze for a minute. Then his eyes became darker than amber, and she knew he was holding a tight rein on his temper. "I see," he said coolly. "You and What's-his name spend a lot of time aboard her now."

"Axel. And we were just going to go out on Sunday," Kathy said. Then she leaped off her bar stool and exploded. "What business is it of yours,

McQueen? You walked away. And you seem to be spending all your time with that little twit—"

"Little twit?"

"Marla Harrington. And twit's your daughter's term, not mine!"

He stared at her as if he was going to explode. Then the darkness left his eyes and a golden flame of humor sizzled in them. "You should hear what she calls your good friend Axel," he warned her.

"What?"

He twisted his jaw and shook his head, silently laughing. "Never mind. Let's go. Call Patty and make sure she'll feed Sam for the next couple of days in case we have trouble finding them."

"You want me to call Patty after—"

"Yes. Tell her you just want to be with Shanna. I'm sure she'll understand."

"But not good enough for me to tell her the truth."

"Dammit, Kathy, I don't want to drag anyone into this if I don't have to. You and Shanna are known quantities in my life. Patty isn't. Don't tell her anything. Then let's go. It's dark. We should be able to get to the docks without being seen. And we'll slip out really quietly. And find Shanna."

She nodded, but she still wasn't moving.

"What's the matter?"

She shook her head. "I just—I just wasn't planning on a cruise with you this evening," she murmured. And certainly not on the *Sweet Eden*, the vessel that had played such a very important part in their lives....

He came close to her, a wicked grin on his lips, and he leaned low to meet her eyes.

"What's the matter, Kath? Frightened of the things going on? Or of me?"

She shook her head, smiling. "Uh-uh."

"Hmm," he murmured. "Maybe you should be. 'Cause you know what, my love? I can still kiss you without thinking that I should throw up, either."

"How sweet. You always did have a way with words."

His smile deepened. "They were your words, remember? Actually, when I kissed you, there were other things I was thinking about. Lots and lots of other things. Maybe we should both be afraid," he said huskily. Then he turned away from her. "Come on. We've really got to go. I need my wallet. Get whatever you need and let's get out of here. I'll lock up the back where I came in through the bathroom. You still have that little secret door for Sam?"

"Uh, yes. He can come in or out if he wants. He usually likes to be out, though."

"Patty has keys?"

She nodded jerkily. "Brent—"

"Kathy, move!"

He was already past her, on his way to the bedroom.

She gritted her teeth. She wanted to fight and argue and deny any time with him at all. She wanted to deny any feeling for him!

But she had to reach her daughter. It was a desperate situation, and he did seem to have it all figured out.

It was just that she was going to go with him. Alone. Aboard the *Sweet Eden*.

A curious warmth snaked along the length of her spine, and for a moment she could barely breathe. She couldn't be alone with him. They'd been apart for three years and she'd barely seen him again and already...

It was almost as if they had never parted. His kiss, his touch, were every bit as evocative, as seductive, as they had ever been.

They'd been apart. They were divorced. Their daughter was at stake. Surely, she could go with him and hold her own.

Surely, she could...

"Kathy!"

It seemed that she jumped a mile at the sound of his voice. She spun. He was at the door, ready, his gaze sharp, his voice commanding.

She could hold her own.

She smiled sweetly at him. She just had to remember that he could be a temperamental, domineering son of a gun, that was all. Then she'd be just fine.

She collected a purse, slipped into a pair of sneakers then hurried to the door. He was there waiting.

"Let's go!" he said impatiently.

She sailed past him, her jaw clenched tight, her smile still in place.

"Fine! Let's go!"

She was holding her own, all right.

She was trembling like a leaf as the warm night air embraced her and they slipped away into the darkness.

# Chapter 3

The moon was full, casting a surreal glow on the stately old houses along the way to the water. There wasn't another soul around as Brent led the way down the dock and leaped aboard the *Sweet Eden*. "Get the ropes, Kath, will you?"

She paused, arching a brow, then decided that she would help cast away without arguing.

The *Sweet Eden* was hers, though. They might have owned it together once, but it was all hers now. Yet he seemed to think he still owned it!

By the time she had tossed the ropes to the deck and jumped aboard, he'd switched on the lights and started the motor. As she moved to take a seat at the helm, she found he had beat her to it.

Not that he wasn't an excellent sailor. He always had been. He loved the water and everything to do with it.

He smiled at her as she approached him. "Have a seat, Kathryn. My God, it's peaceful out here, isn't it?"

Kathy sat on the curve of the seat beside him. The *Sweet Eden* was a nicely shaped and compact sailboat with all the pleasures of home—well, almost all the pleasures. There was no gigantic bath aboard. The heads were small and compact. The helm was situated at the rear with topside space for about ten people. Down a flight of six steps were the galley, dining area and two cabins, one portside and one starboard. Each had a tiny head with a toilet, shower and sink.

Despite the fact that there was plenty of space between them, Kathy sat gingerly on the edge of the padded fiberglass seat. "It's quiet because very few people go on pleasure cruises at this time of night."

"Really?" he drawled.

"Mmm. And would you like me to take over? It is a little tricky here out to the bay—"

"I'm fine."

"It's been three years—"

"Kathy, I've done this hundreds of times. I know what I'm doing."

"It's my boat!"

His teeth flashed white in the shadows of the night. "So it is, Ms. O'Hara. Indulge me."

She threw up her hands. "Indulge you? Brent, I'm indulging the hell out of you as it is! Think about it. We haven't exchanged a single word in three years and the next thing I know you're in my bathtub."

"My bathtub, too."

"Your use of the facilities for bubble baths was not in the agreement!" Kathy reminded him indignantly. "Nor do I owe you this, any of this. I'm not even sure if I agree with what we're doing! And at the very least, you might want to recall, Brent, you walked out on me!"

"You filed for the divorce."

"You left—"

He exploded suddenly with a long, passionate oath, his fingers winding white-knuckled and tense over the wheel. "We'd lost one child and I'd caused you to lose another. How the hell long was I supposed to stay?"

Kathy gasped and leaped to her feet, stunned by the fury and passion—and the anguish—of his words. This was a mistake. There was nothing left between them except for old wounds. Agonizing wounds, barely sutured, that bled at the slightest brush.

"You're right!" she snapped. "There was nothing to stay for, nothing at all."

Tears were nearly blinding her. She left him and hurried below. He did know what he was doing. He could fend for himself.

She entered the first cabin and fell upon the bunk, clenching her teeth hard to hold the emotions surging inside her at bay. She didn't want to remember, she hated to remember. Maybe it had all started with the television today, maybe Brent's last words really had very little to do with it. But it was all there, rushing over her.

Ryan had been so little. Just two months old. And they had tried for him for so long, Kathy becoming concerned, Brent telling her that trying was the most fun in the whole world. And then they'd had him and he'd been the most beautiful little boy in the world, with huge blue eyes and dark blond curls, and they'd all adored him, Shanna included. But then the night had come when he should have started crying at his feeding time and Kathy had lain there awake smiling, just waiting. She waited and waited, then she got up and walked down the hall to his room and to his crib. She found him lying on his stomach, his little rump up in the air, as he slept so very often.

But when she reached for him, he was cold. So cold. She turned him over and his tiny lips were blue, and it was then that she started to scream.

In seconds Brent was down the hall and in the room. He shocked her into action and between them, they tried to revive him while Shanna called 911.

There was nothing anyone could do. It was infant death syndrome, the doctor explained, so tragic, a horrible loss, and only God could understand. And she had cried and cried and hated God with all her might, and Brent, immersed in the loss, had held her. He'd been the rock she so desperately needed.

It was only later that she began to lose him, and she never saw it. Maybe she had begun to lash out first, maybe she'd been trying to crawl out of the lonely well of pain. Maybe she had wanted to fight because fighting made her feel as if they were still alive...

"Kathy."

She started, amazed to see him silhouetted in the doorway. She hadn't turned on the cabin lights, and they were in darkness and shadow. She realized the engine had stopped.

"Brent—"

"It's all right. We're hugging the coast and I'm anchored."

"You're sure—"

"Kathy, I'm sure. Honestly, I do know what I'm doing." She could see the flash of his rueful smile in the darkness. "Maybe I haven't been aboard this boat in a while, but I have been on others."

Yes, he had. He'd been fishing in the video, with Marla Harrington draped all over him.

He took a step into the room and sat on the bunk beside her. Before she could stop him, before she realized what he was doing, he reached out and touched her cheek, then rubbed his fingers together after finding the dampness there. Quickly she wiped away the tears.

"Kathy, I'm sorry, really sorry."

She wanted to speak quickly. She wanted to escape the close confines of the cabin. She didn't want him so near, and she didn't want him touching her because it all felt so natural and so right. She wanted him so badly, wanted to be held in his arms, wanted his kiss, wanted his naked body next to hers, wanted to make love...

And it wouldn't be right. It would be very, very wrong. It hadn't been a casual affair that had ended, maybe to be resumed again. It had been their whole lives, and their lives had been shattered, and she wasn't playing with that kind of fire ever again.

"It's all right, Brent."

"You're crying."

"It's not your fault."

"It is, and it was."

"No, it was nobody's fault, remember? That's what they said."

"Kathy, I didn't mean to do this to you, I just wanted to get you and Shanna to safety. Want to try to start over for the evening?"

What else was there to do? She couldn't go home because they still had to find their daughter. And she couldn't stay in the cabin because she would throw her arms around him and burst into tears and beg him to make love to her just one more time, and give her one more memory to live on during the empty years to follow.

If they survived this, she thought fleetingly, then pushed the thought furiously away.

They would survive. She'd make Brent be careful, if nothing else. If he was going to make them go away, she was going to make him go away, too, she decided firmly.

"Dinner," she breathed.

"Pardon?"

"You said that you wanted to start the night over. All right, you muscled your way to the helm. Want to muscle your way to the galley?"

"Sure." He stood, reached down a hand to her and pulled her to her feet. Then he paused for a moment and she thought her heart stopped beating, that the whole world and time had ceased to exist. She thought he was going to touch her again, to say something, but he did not. He left the cabin and strode down the aisle to the galley.

"All right, Ms. O'Hara, what am I cooking?"

"I'm not sure," she admitted. She opened the tiny refrigerator behind the carved oak counter and started looking through the provisions. "Omelets!" she said at last. She set a dozen eggs on the stainless steel counter by the sink then began adding other ingredients. "Mushrooms, peppers, onions, cheese, sausage—"

"Hold up on the sausage, Ms. O'Hara," he instructed her. "That must be for the new love of your life. I detest sausage, remember?"

He spoke lightly but there was an edge to his voice. And when she glanced at him, he was leaning over the counter, watching her, a golden light glistening in his eyes. She hadn't forgotten the danger signals. She smiled sweetly, wondering why she felt such a rush of excitement at his anger. Was he jealous? If so, it was damned nice. He hadn't a thing to be jealous about, but he didn't know that. "Sorry," she told him casually. "I guess I did forget."

"Do you have any normal beer in there?" he asked her.

"Normal beer?"

"Good old American brew. Instead of your, er, friend's trendy water?"

Shanna had done some of the stocking of the galley, and all her life, she had stocked it with her father's favorites. Kathy tossed Brent a beer.

"Thanks. I guess memory does survive at times."

"In your daughter's heart."

"So is he much of a sailor?" Brent asked politely.

"He's fine."

"Just fine? I would have thought that you would have demanded so much more out of life."

"We were talking about sailing."

"Were we? I had the impression we were talking about something else. Everything about him seems to be fine. Not good, not great, not wonderful. Just fine. You ought to be shooting for wonderful, Kathy."

"Ah. Because you were wonderful?" she challenged him.

He smiled, his lip curving slowly. He bent close to her and lifted a lock of her hair, then slowly let it go. "Yeah. At some things. We were pretty wonderful."

She pulled away from him, bumping her head against the cabinets. He started to reach for her, worried, and she pulled away again. "I'm fine! It's okay. Hey, you're supposed to be doing the cooking remember."

"Yeah, sure."

He sipped his beer, set the can on the counter and started to rummage through the cabinets. "Where the heck is the frying pan?"

"Amazing, isn't it? You remember the docks and the ships and everything else—but not where the pans are kept!" Deciding they were never going to eat if she didn't get him started, Kathy found the large frying pan and a cutting board. Brent managed to find some butter in the refrigerator, then the bread basket, and while she chopped peppers and mushrooms and onions, he cut slices of bread. As long as she was busy with the work before her, her eyes on her chopping, she thought she could manage a few queries.

"So tell me, Brent. How about you? Is Marla... just wonderful?"

He made a grunting sound. "Marla isn't anything at all," he told her briefly.

"Whoops. Trouble in paradise?" she asked sweetly.

He cast her a glance. "Where are you getting your information?" he asked her. "If you've been reading those rag magazines, you should recall that they once had a story about the two of us breaking up because you were having an affair with an Arab prince."

She had to smile, the story had been so ridiculous. They had both laughed over it, wondered whether to sue or not. Then Brent's lawyer had demanded a retraction and it had been given.

Kathy tossed the peppers into a little glass bowl and started on the mushrooms. "No, I haven't been reading rag magazines. I only read the front pages in the supermarket, and I try to refrain from reading about you at all."

"Do you?" he asked wickedly. "You mean you're never just the slightest bit interested in what I'm up to?"

"Nope," Kathy said, meeting his eyes, tossing a handful of mushrooms into the bowl.

"Ah, yes, that's because you're so involved with Mr. Fine."

"He's a very considerate man."

"That must be exciting."

"Not as exciting as Marla Harrington, I'm sure."

He sipped his beer again and leaned over the counter, watching her. "So what do you know about Marla? And if you're not interested, why do you know anything?"

"We share a child, remember?"

"I see. So what did our shared child tell you?"

"Just that she's a twit," Kathy said sweetly.

"What makes you think I'm involved with the twit?" he asked.

"Well, if you're not involved with the twit, she's involved with you. She was draped all over you like curtains in that video."

He started to laugh, straightening. She cast him a glance and nearly chopped off her fingertip. "It's nice to see you still have claws!" he told her.

"I haven't," she denied.

"But that sounds like such a jealous comment!"

"It's not jealous at all. It's just a comment."

"And you don't read anything about me, but you did see the video."

"What did you want me to say to your daughter when she insisted that I come out to see it? She's very proud of you, you know. And I've never discouraged that."

He was silent for a second, then she felt his eyes again, very warm upon her. "I know," he said huskily.

Again, it seemed that the space around them was too tight, that he was too close. She could smell a hint of his after-shave, feel the warmth of his body. It was so easy to let the years apart disappear, to pretend that this was like many a voyage they had taken, to imagine that she could drop what she was doing, forget the omelet, cry out and throw her arms around him, and damn everything else.

"So," she said quickly, desperate to break the spell, "is it on or off with you and Marla?"

"Marla? Not the twit?"

"Even twits have names," she said pleasantly.

"It was never on," he said.

"You should tell that to Marla."

"I have."

"I think she's in love with you."

"All that from a video?" he demanded. "Are you sure you haven't been reading rag magazines?"

She smiled. "Women don't drape that way unless they're in love."

"It was a video. She was acting."

"She is a ... friend, though, I take it?"

"I met her through the Hicks brothers. They always have lots and lots of friends around them. Why don't you just come right out and ask me what you want to know."

She gazed at him, startled. "And what is it that I want to know?"

"If I'm sleeping with her or not."

She kept staring at him. She wanted to tell him she could care less who he was sleeping with. "All right," she said blandly. "Are you sleeping with her?"

He picked up a piece of pepper and popped it into his mouth. "No, and I never was. My turn. Are you sleeping with Mr. So-so?"

"Brent, that's none of your—"

"Are you?"

She exhaled. "I—no."

He smiled and turned away, coming around the counter to pick up the eggs. He broke them into a large bowl. "I'm glad," he said quietly.

"Oh? Was I supposed to remain celibate forever?"

"Hardly," he said, whipping up the eggs. "But if you're going to have an affair, it should be a lot better than just fine."

"Thanks. I think." She hesitated. He'd turned on a burner and begun to cook. Once he'd flipped the omelet he glanced up to find her staring at him.

"What?" he demanded.

"I was just wondering about the rest of your life."

"What about it?"

"Oh. Just what you've been doing with it."

"And who I've been doing it with?"

"It's really none of my business, is it?"

He offered her a crooked smile, lowered his lashes and slid the omelet onto a plate without answering. He poured in the remaining mixture. "My life is rather at a stalemate," he told her.

She didn't say anything, but picked up the plate along with napkins and silverware and asked, "Want to eat topside?"

"Sure. There's a great moon out there tonight." He was still staring at the frying pan, and still grinning, she thought. Then his eyes rose to hers. "You're not afraid to be with me, up there, in all that moonlight, are you?"

"Have you taken up turning into a wolf during the full moon?" Kathy asked. Then, before he could reply, she answered herself. "Never mind. You always were a wolf by the full moon. And any other moon, at that."

"Not always."

"Oh?"

"It depends on the available prey," he told her.

"Ah, I see. Where do ex-wives fit in?"

"I've only got one," he reminded her.

"So?"

"It kind of depends on the ex-wife," he said. He flipped the omelet, slipped it onto a plate and smiled innocently at her. "What are you drinking, Ms. O'Hara? Wine cooler or a foreign beer?"

"A domestic beer will be fine, thank you, Mr. McQueen," she said sweetly, then quickly preceded him up the steps. She felt the warm breeze touch her, and she was instantly aware of the moon. It was very full, glowing with a soft shimmer over the water. The *Sweet Eden* rocked gently at anchor. Across the lightly rippling waves, Kathy could see the lights of the shoreline. It was a beautiful view, stunning. And they were all alone within it. She couldn't see another boat anywhere. There was nothing to see except for the lights on the shore, the velvet darkness of the sky and the beauty of the moon and the stars. And there was the water, too, seemingly eternal. The shoreline was the only touch of civilization, and it seemed a long way away.

She perched on the padded fiberglass bench, and in another moment, Brent was with her. He sat down on the curve of the seat, so that they weren't touching, and yet they weren't very far apart. He offered her a beer and she silently passed him a fork and napkin in return.

"What a stunning night," he murmured.

She nodded, watching the stars. "Where would you be, Brent, if you weren't here?" she asked him impulsively.

"What?" he asked softly.

"If you weren't so worried about Shanna. Where would you be, what would you be doing tonight?"

"I thought you weren't really so interested in my life."

"What would you be doing?" she repeated.

He shrugged. "Well, I was supposed to be meeting with Johnny, remember? And I was supposed to be meeting Robert, so I would have been doing one of those two things."

"And if not meeting with people?" Kathy persisted.

He smiled. "This particular Saturday night I was invited to be out with Shanna and David and his parents."

"You were!" Kathy exclaimed. "I was invited, too."

"And Shanna probably knew that neither of us could come."

"Well, actually, David invited me. Shanna didn't want me to come because—" She broke off.

"Because of What's-his-name, right?"

"Axel," she said dryly, "and I could swear that you do remember that name."

"Maybe." He finished his eggs and set the plate aside, stretching his arms across the seat and sitting back comfortably. "Speaking of Mr. Fine, where were you and he supposedly headed tonight?"

"Dinner."

"Ah, dinner."

"Yes, it's a meal you eat at night."

"And I'm sure he does it very well. Only in the best restaurants. He probably speaks French with a very American accent but likes to impress his dates by using the language to order wine, right?"·

Kathy put down her plate, feeling her temper sizzle. It didn't help one bit that what he was saying was the truth, right to the bone. She stood and stared at him, her hands on her hips. "At least he never walked out on me."

"What?"

It was a mistake to be sarcastic, she quickly realized, a mistake to give away the least emotion—because he was up and on his feet, too, and staring her down.

"Dammit, I never just walked out on you!"

She spun around and grabbed the plates and started down to the galley. He was right on her heels. "Kathy, don't walk away. I'm trying to talk to you."

"I tried to talk once, too," she snapped. He wasn't going to leave her, he was right behind her, watching her every move. She'd meant to wash the plates, but he was too close, so she hurried up the steps.

And he was still right behind her. He was going to touch her. She turned, her fingers clenched at her sides, staring at him. "I don't want to talk anymore, Brent. We had that argument and when I wanted to try to understand it, you were gone! So don't start with me—"

Abruptly she turned off the water and groped for a towel on the nearby rack. Then she dried herself briskly and opened the dresser door in one of the built-in cabinets.

She stared blankly at the emptiness there before remembering that she had moved all of her clothing into the other cabin when she had planned the outing with Axel. This was the nicest cabin, and she had wanted to offer it to her guest.

She stood, perplexed, certain that she didn't want to go walk out clad only in the wisp of a towel. Then she looked at the door and exhaled with a certain relief because she had a terry robe hanging there. It wasn't great, but it was better than a towel. In fact, lots of women probably felt fairly well covered in a floor-length terry robe.

But they were women who didn't know Brent, who didn't already feel as if their flesh and blood and limbs were already half afire, women who didn't feel as if they were already touched, already naked, waiting...

She wrenched open the cabin door and stood in the narrow hallway. She couldn't hear a shower running so she hesitated, then knocked on the door.

It was thrown open, and there was Brent, in a wisp of a towel himself, his dark blond hair slicked back from the shower, an expression of irritability naked on his face. "I see that you did clean out in here," he said curtly.

"What?"

"I can't find a thing in here to wear."

"It's my boat! And you've been out of my life for three years!"

"Any suggestions?" he asked her.

"Yes! Yes, I've lots and lots of suggestions for you but I'm really not certain that you want to hear them!" She flared. "Yes, I've dozens of suggestions! You could start out by locking yourself in a closet!"

"Kathy, you little brat—"

He didn't get any further. She shoved her hands against his chest, thrusting him into the room, then she swung around almost blindly, wanting to escape him once again.

She didn't hear him behind her as she passed the galley and mounted the steps. She didn't sense him until his hands were on her and he was spinning her around. She cried out and fell down to the floor beneath him.

He was sprawled over her, taut, tense, his chest naked and the muscles rippling. The moon glowed on the bronze of his flesh, the harsh constriction in his features. His eyes seemed to blaze gold, searing her. "Kathy!" he began, then fell silent. Then he groaned as his fingers moved into her hair . . . and he was kissing her.

Not as he had kissed her earlier. Not lightly, not tauntingly. But with hunger, raw and ravenous.

Open-mouthed, his lips moved upon hers, wet, hot, eliciting. His tongue swept her mouth, thrust, demanded, tasted and thrust even deeper. Then he drew away and his lips touched her face. His tongue rimmed her lips before slipping inside her mouth again, so deeply that the heat and fever spread throughout her body. His fingers were in her hair, but there was no pain, even though he held her so tautly because of his need. She didn't want to touch him . . . but her fingers were upon his shoulders.

She didn't want to feel the warmth of his body, didn't want to recognize the length of it, the hardness of his thighs, the tautness of his belly . . . the bulge of his desire. She didn't want to feel the overwhelming urge, the fire, the desperation to have him at the cost of peace and sanity and life itself.

She didn't want to . . .

His lips rose above hers just a fraction of an inch. She touched them delicately with her tongue, encircling them, nipping lightly. He held still to her gentle assault, then swept his arms around her. Once again their mouths melded and the tasting and sweeping and hunger were shared. When they broke apart again, his hold on her hair eased, but the tension in him seemed even greater, explosive, anguished. His breath fanning her cheeks, he whispered, "Kathy, I didn't mean it to come to this. The last thing I ever wanted to do was hurt you again. And by God, I sure as hell didn't want to do this to myself!"

She lay still, thinking that he couldn't mean it, that he couldn't manage to walk away now. The kiss was a mistake, but she'd live with the mistake, she swore silently. She'd live with the agony of all the tomorrows...

If she could just have this moment beneath the black velvet darkness of the sky and the ethereal glow of the silver full moon.

He was standing, reaching down to her, helping her to her feet. She stared at him, her fingers still entwined with his, her lips swollen and soft and wet from the kiss.

"Brent!" She whispered his name. He didn't speak, and his eyes remained hard upon hers. "It's a mistake, I know it's a mistake..." Her voice trailed away miserably. She knew him still, knew him so well. But he wasn't hers any more, and she wondered if his desire was great enough, if she could seduce him, if she wasn't making a fool of herself again.

"What, Kathy, what?" His voice was nearly a growl, his words fraught with tension.

She shook her head and tried to whisper more softly. "It's a mistake, but...maybe it's not a mistake. Maybe we can just touch and then let go. I mean by the light of day we can turn aside, we can see all the truths, we can know that it's over, that we can't take the pain again. But I was just thinking that tonight..."

She freed her fingers from his. She couldn't go on any longer, not without some help. She stepped back and turned around, her cheeks flushed with embarrassment, her back to him.

He was silent. She felt the cool night breeze sweep around her and heard its soft whisper. She listened to the gentle lapping of the water against the hull of the boat.

Then he stepped toward her, and she felt his hands upon her shoulders.

The terry robe that had never seemed much of a barrier went sliding to the deck at her feet, and she felt the searing fire of his lips against her naked shoulder.

## Chapter 4

Kathy caught her breath as she felt the touch of the night breeze combine with the caress of his kiss against her flesh. He lifted her hair and pressed his lips to her nape, and his kiss moved once more over her shoulder blades. She stood naked in the moonlight, thinking that they had never made love quite like this. She felt as if she should drape something around her, but then she felt the eternity of the night and the stars and the sea, and it suddenly seemed the most private place in the world, just as his touch with that of the night wind seemed to be the most sensual she had ever felt.

His arms swept around her from behind and she felt the erotic brush of the golden mat of his chest hair against her back. His hands swept upward, encircling her breasts, cupping them tenderly, his thumbs moving in seductive rhythm over her nipples.

Then his kisses began to move down the length of her spine. Slowly his lips moved, touching each and every vertebra. Warm moisture burned her flesh, then the liquid fire was enhanced by the coolness of the breeze. Finally he was on his knees behind her, his fingers brushing her belly, his lips teasing her buttocks. Then she gasped as he turned her around. His face and hair lay buried against her abdomen, and the soft flick of his tongue began to touch her there. His hands stroked downward, over her hips and calves, then swept up her kneecaps and upper thighs, until she parted her stance for balance. He held her taut against him, and his searing, moist caress moved over the apex of her limbs, to the intimate center of her desire.

Three years were nothing....

The sensations that ripped through her were wild and sweetly primeval, as natural as the swell of the waves in the sea. She felt a raging ecstasy so swift and overwhelming that nothing else existed. Her fingers tore into his hair but she did not seek to pull him away, only to hold tight lest the storm of desire send her spiraling into darkness. He brought her ever closer, ever more intimately against him. And he parted her further with his touch, stroking her endlessly. Torrents of pleasure, wilder than any tempest on the ocean, came sweeping through her and she twisted and moaned. The sweet liquid fire simmering deep within her rose and rose, until it burst explosively, until she did see darkness, and came sinking down slowly before him, spent, exhausted, emptied. Then brilliant lights and sparks of fire seemed to cascade around her. She closed her eyes, still shaking, and embraced him, her lashes lowered. A rosy color crept into her cheeks because she had responded so uninhibitedly to his intimate touch after so many years had passed.

But he didn't allow her any regrets. He caught her lips and kissed her deeply and passionately, slowly lowering them to the deck. He whispered to her decadently, demanding to know if she could taste the love between them on their kiss. Before she could regain her senses from the first explosion, he had slipped inside her. He was magnificent, and just feeling him inside her as he whispered so erotically brought her near to a second climax before he even started to move his body.

Then he did so, languidly, nearly leaving, then entering her again deeply. The quickening deepened inside her again; the sparks of fire left behind were incredibly fanned. As he held his weight above her carefully on the palms of his hands, their only contact being where his body was immersed so deeply within her own, she began to meet his slow, demanding thrusts.

The world took flight all over again. As he moved within her he leaned down and took the hardened peak of her nipple into his mouth, and he sucked it hard as the speed of his rhythm increased to a frantic beat. She clung to him. She bit and kissed his shoulders, she pushed her fingers into his hair.

Then it seemed that the sky exploded above her, and the darkness was filled with myriad multicolored stars and lights. The exquisite pleasure of her body was seeping into his while he held still, emptying the tempest of his own desire deep within her.

Then he fell by her side, gasping, and she fought to regain her breath, her sanity and her reason.

She didn't know what to do or what to say as she lay sheened with sweat, glistening in the moonlight. Hundreds of little things she had seen in the movies swept through her mind, but she knew none of them was right. Was it good for you? It was magnificent for me. No, no, those were things that strangers said, or near strangers, and they were not strangers. But neither was he her husband any more, nor could this magic last. It had been stolen, a few snatched moments.

Still it seemed that something should be said, but not the truth. She would babble. My God, I didn't remember just how sweet, how wonderful, how shattering, how volatile making love with you is. How it could make the entire world seem to disappear, and I wonder, is it because I'm still in love with you, or are you really such an incredible lover?

And maybe it's both...

It wasn't going to be awkward, and it wasn't going to be hard, she realized. He wasn't going to let it be so.

His arm came around her, pulling her close beside him. He brushed a kiss against her forehead and held her beneath the stars. She stared at the stars as the silence stretched between them, then he spoke. There was a husky trembling to his voice that seemed to reach inside her and squeeze her heart. "Kathy, I remember so much, and yet...God, I've missed you."

She smiled slightly and buried her face against his ribs, slightly stroking his naked belly. "I've missed you," she admitted softly. Then she sighed, because she was so replete. She didn't want to move, and she really didn't want to talk any more, not that night. She didn't want the past to intrude, she didn't want to remember any of the pain. She just wanted to lie there, beneath the stars, secure in his embrace, and remember what it had been like when he had loved her, too, when he had really been hers to love.

But she inhaled on a shaky breath and said, "We should go."

To her surprise and pleasure, she felt him shake his head. "It must be one o'clock by now. Even if we managed to catch up with them in the next few hours, we'd probably wake everyone up and scare them all half to death. We'll start out at first light.''

''Oh,'' she murmured. Her heart was thundering. She didn't want to move. And he didn't move. She felt his lightest touch, and the touch of the breeze, moving over her naked flesh. She closed her eyes. She had slept so many nights of her life in his arms, just like this. It was all new, and yet it was all so familiar. . . .

She must have closed her eyes and dozed. She was vaguely aware that he dragged the cushions down from the fiberglass seats and that he laid her upon them. Sometime during the night he must have gone down to one of the cabins, because a sheet was wrapped around them both, a gentle barrier against the slight coolness of the breeze.

When she awoke, the stars were still in the sky, but the darkness was fading fast. The dawn was coming in curious, soft pastel shades. A filter of pink was stretching across the heavens before any touch of the sun's gold.

Brent was still sleeping. His bare back was to her; the sheet had fallen from his shoulders. She stared at the breadth of his muscles, and she felt like smiling just because she liked the way he was built. His back was bronzed from the sun, and it tapered to a narrow waistline. Below that his flesh was a lighter shade, and his buttocks were rounded and hard-muscled and very sexy, she thought. She wanted to reach out and touch him. Despite the fact that so much had been drained from her the night before, that so much desire had exploded with such tremendous force, she wanted to taste his flesh. See if it was salty, if . . .

He turned his head suddenly, and she realized that he was awake. His heavy-lidded golden gaze was upon her with a certain amount of amusement. She met his gaze, then moved toward him. Her lashes fell at the very last instant, as she touched his flesh with her lips, then grazed it slightly with her teeth. He didn't move; he waited. But she was certain she felt the beat of his heart, felt his pulse at his nape, felt the intake of his breath, the hardening of his body.

As he had done the night before, she began to move against him. She kissed the breadth of his back, caressing it with her fingers. She teased his spine, up and down, with the moist pink flicker of her tongue. She caressed the small of his back and nipped at his buttocks and bathed them with her kiss.

He rolled to his side, and she was face to face with his hardness, the result of her assault. She felt a delicious power surge through her with an unbearable sweetness as she realized that she could still affect him as deeply as he could her. But it wasn't just with that sense of power that she continued to touch him, it was also with love, with memory. Once he had been hers. And on this shimmering pink morning, he was going to be hers again.

She closed her fingers around him, teased and caressed him and stroked him with her tongue. She heard his ragged cries, and the molten fire took hold within her own body. A fever began to rule her movements. She tasted his ecstasy, and still she held him with her caress, until his hands were on her and he was lifting her and she discovered herself seated on one of the fiberglass benches. His hands were upon her, parting her thighs. His eyes were glittering with passion. Then he began his own assault, searing her to her very center with the hot thrust of his tongue, then rising to impale her and take her with reckless fury. Cries tore from their throats, and spasms shook them as they peaked in an exultant climax together.

He held her very close, burying his face against her hair and throat. "I had forgotten how nice it could be to wake up beside you," he said softly.

To wake up...

It was morning, and there was no more darkness to use as a shield against the past. She had wanted him, and she had had him, but it had been a horrible mistake. No matter how deeply she had been filled, she was still hungry. Their union wasn't as complete as she had thought it would be.

She had wanted a memory. And in the light of day, the pain from the past would come back. Sex had never been their problem. It was life that had come between them. It had been his temper, and her temper, and the awful things they had said. Nothing could erase the things that had happened.

"We have to go," she whispered painfully.

He nodded.

She started to rise, but he pulled her back, his eyes questioning as they touched her. "Kathy, tell me, are you sorry?"

She wanted to pull away. She didn't want to answer a question like that.

But he wasn't going to let her go.

"I don't know, Brent. I really don't know. It was probably the biggest mistake either of us has ever made. And—" She broke off, then she inhaled quickly and lowered her lashes. "That's all a lie. Maybe not all a lie. No, I'm not sorry. I wanted you last night more than I can remember ever wanting anything or anyone."

"What about this morning?" he demanded.

"I . . . wanted you this morning."

He inhaled quickly and seemed to catch his breath. He looked at ease and very handsome, sitting naked on the fiberglass by the hull. Was she so natural and easy, standing there in the buff, now in the sun and the early morning light? She tugged his hand. "Brent, it's daylight. Fishermen will be coming out."

He smiled. "You look great."

"Thank you."

"You always did."

"Thank you. So, uh, so do you. Brent, let go, please, we've got to get clothes on."

He shook his head, holding her tight. "Uh-uh. Not yet."

"What do you want?" she demanded desperately.

"I don't want to pretend that it didn't happen, that's all."

"I never meant to pretend."

"Or that it wasn't good, Kathy. And I don't mean that in any casual way. It was good for the past, and good for the future, and when I'm with you, you have to know that I want you."

She tugged more desperately on his hand. "Brent, we're not going to be together, remember? It's too damned dangerous. And not because of Johnny Blondell."

He dropped her hand slowly, and his eyes were heavily shaded as they brushed hers once again. "That's right. Damned right," he said coolly. He rose, relaxed again, able to swing in the breeze with the best composure. "Let's shower and get going. I'm really sorry. I guess I did forget some of the past."

He walked past her and disappeared into the cabin. She held still a second longer, wanting to scream. He didn't understand. He didn't understand what she had been trying to say at all. "Oh,

Brent!'' she said to the breeze. There were tears on her cheeks. She wiped them away furiously. She had taken what she wanted, and now it was time to pay. She'd made her bargain with herself openly, knowing the consequences.

She hurried down the steps to her cabin and into the shower. She turned on the water and leaned against the wall.

He thought he had hurt her, and he thought he was going to hurt her again.

The water poured softly on her and she leaned there, trying to reason, trying to understand herself.

He thought he had caused her to lose the new baby that had meant so very much to them both after Ryan had died. He had thought that the argument had caused her miscarriage, that he had been too rough, that he couldn't give what she needed anymore. And she had been too hurt herself at the time to realize he was slipping away with every remote, polite word. He had moved out of the house, and he hadn't been able to talk to her. Her pain had turned to fury and she had filed papers, and suddenly all that had been left was the pain.

He hadn't left when she had been sick. He had been there, white-faced, every day. He hadn't left her alone for a minute in the hospital, not when she had hemorrhaged, not when she had hovered so dangerously on the line between life and death. She could remember trying to promise him that there would be another son, and she had thought then that he was bitterly disappointed because he had seemed to decide, all on his own, that there never would be another one.

When Ryan had died, he had been tender at first. Then he had dragged her back into life, and that had included arguing—and making love fiercely, desperately. It had been good for her. She had wanted to live again, but then she had found out that she was pregnant again.

Kathy sank down slowly in the shower stall. He had never realized she hadn't wanted his temper to change. They had been wild as kids, neither one of them willing to give up a battle, and yet neither one of them walking away.

They had argued right down the aisle, so it seemed.

And he thought it was his temper. The doctor couldn't convince him that things just happened. She could remember now the way he had listened, his face so taut, his words betraying nothing, the denial within his heart.

"It is the past!" she whispered vehemently. Then she stood, wondering what in hell they were doing. They were forgetting their surviving child, the daughter that meant everything in the world to both of them.

She wrapped up in her towel and hurriedly opened the door to tap on the one across the narrow hallway. There was no answer. She didn't hear the water running so she carefully cracked open the door, then entered the cabin. Brent was gone. Within a few minutes she had pulled out a pair of shorts and a sleeveless cotton shirt with a mandarin collar. She paused as she dressed, listening.

Brent had already brought in the anchor and started the motor.

She walked across the hallway and crawled into the bunk, balancing with just her toes on the bed, to dig into the wall cabinets above it. She had a few things left that belonged to Brent. Cutoffs and old T-shirts. She'd kept them because, with a boat, you never knew when you would need something dry for a guest, male or female.

Maybe that was a lie. Maybe she'd kept them for the same reason she'd kept so many of his things at the house. She hadn't been able to part with them.

Leaving the clothing on the bunk, she hurried out to the galley, then paused. Before going topside she put on a pot of coffee and quickly cleaned up the mess from the night before. She wondered if she was stalling, if she was afraid to see Brent after everything that had passed between them. No, she determined, and hurried topside.

The magical pink lights of the dawn had faded. It was still early, but full daylight was already upon them.

She broke off because his eyes were on her, hard, cold, disdaining. "You think that what happened to Johnny Blondell is silly?"

"No, of course not! But even if we say that something is going on, I still don't understand—"

"Okay, Kathy, listen carefully. Several years ago we were all together as a group, touring South and Central America and the States. We came through customs and Harry Robertson was arrested. The rest of us were furious because musicians seem to get a bad rap to begin with and because—to the best of my knowledge—no one else had had anything to do with it and we all had our private lives, our families and our careers. I felt kind of sorry for Harry because he wouldn't talk, and because he seemed so afraid, and I remember thinking Harry had been coerced into what he was doing. We couldn't really help Harry, no one could. He went to prison—he died in prison. Then Larry Jenkins was killed. Then Keith's wife was killed. Then Johnny Blondell was killed. It seems to me that someone out there thinks we all know something about something, and either they want information no one has been able to give them yet, or they just want anyone who might have any information to be out of the picture. I don't want to use a radio. I don't want anyone to know where Shanna is, I don't want to lead anyone to her."

"Brent, maybe you should be worrying about Marla Harrington."

He cast her a glance that sent daggers. "Why?"

"Well, most people would assume that you were involved with her now, I would think."

He kept watching her. The wind ruffled his drying hair, and he shrugged. "These people aren't fools. Whoever is doing this is not small time, and not a fool."

"But we're divorced—"

"Yes, we're divorced. The only people who have ever been my family, who could be used as a threat against me, who have really mattered in my life, are you and Shanna. A divorce doesn't change the past, Kathy. Whoever is up to this surely knows that."

Despite their tone, his words thrilled her deep inside. Maybe they couldn't put together the pieces of their lives, but it was exciting, it was wonderful, to hear him say that she was the only woman who had ever really mattered.

"Besides," he added curtly, somewhat dispelling the moment, "we were married at the time. And you were with me during a part of that tour. You could be a target yourself. I want you and Shanna out of it as fast as possible."

"So what are you going to do with us?" Kathy inquired sweetly. "I own a business, remember."

"Patty will run your business for the next few days."

"Where will I be?"

"I'm going to take you both out to a private airstrip and get you flown far away."

"We haven't got our passports."

"I've got a pilot friend who's going to take you to a retreat in rural Virginia."

"With some kind of security, I imagine."

He nodded. Then he grinned at her. "I've given a lot of support to one of the senators there and he's going to see to it that you've got lots of protection."

She threw up her hands. "This is crazy, Brent! You don't know what is going on. You have no idea of how long it's going to go on—"

"It doesn't matter how long it goes on!" he snapped savagely.

"And what are you going to do?"

"Go back. I have to."

"So this maniac can blow you up, too?"

"So we don't all have to spend the rest of our lives looking over our shoulders."

She rose irritably. Maybe he was making sense, she couldn't tell anymore. But she didn't want to go to rural Virginia and be a prisoner.

Maybe that wasn't it. She was very frightened for her daughter, and she did want Shanna in safe hiding as soon as possible. She just didn't want to go herself. She didn't want Brent playing cat and mouse, alone, with murderers. Maybe he wouldn't be alone. Keith Montgomery and the Hicks brothers were still alive and well—and maybe targets, too.

If Brent went to the police, they'd have protection in Miami. And in Miami they had Sam, and her walled estate, and the alarm system.

They. . .

She didn't know if he meant to go to the house. He had his own big place on the water, with studio equipment and everything he needed. He didn't have Sam, though. He would need Sam.

"I'm not sure about this at all, Brent," she told him.

"What do you mean, you're not sure about this?" he exploded. "You've got to do exactly what I'm telling you."

"Oh, no, I don't. We're divorced, remember. I can do whatever I please."

"Kathy—"

"Brent!"

He looked as if he was about to leap for her throat. The tiller lay between them.

He clenched his teeth. She saw him fight for control. "Kathy," he said her name very softly. "You are the most stubborn and obstinate and argumentative woman I have ever met. But you are going to do what I ask you this time, even if I have to tie you hand and foot and mail you north in a box."

He wasn't going to lose his temper. He was going to try damned hard not to lose his temper.

She lowered her head, suddenly aware that she wanted him really angry. She wanted him to leap for her, and she wanted the fight and the passion, and she wanted him to know...

She felt warm, flushed, and she realized that she wanted something very much like that last argument between them. She wanted the furious, cutting words, she wanted the tempest....

And she wanted him to grab her and carry her away and make love to her with that same fury and passion. It was the only way he would ever understand that he hadn't hurt her. But maybe the pieces couldn't be put back together again.

Last night had put the longing and the passion and the sweetness and magic back into her heart when she had tried so hard to forget it had all existed. And now, this morning, there was all the anguish again.

She didn't want to hurt him....

Yes, she did. She wanted to shake him, and she wanted to make him see that he had been wrong. She wanted him to understand that she had been bleeding deep inside, and that had been why she had filed the papers against him, not because she had ever believed for a minute that what had happened had been his fault.

"We'll see," she said sweetly.

"I mean what I'm saying."

"Are you threatening me?"

"I'm just telling you the situation. Take that however you want to take it."

"Maybe I've got my own ideas on what should be done, and how it should be done, Brent."

"Damn you, Kathy, you would try the patience of a saint."

"And you sure as hell aren't any saint, right?"

"Kathy—"

She leaned close to him and smiled sweetly. "Get this, Brent. I'll decide what to do with my own life and you haven't got a single say in it, understand?"

A golden, furious fire leaped into his eyes. She heard the grinding of his teeth and she knew he was going to reach out and wrap his fingers around her arm.

She moved just in time. "I am going to have more coffee. Let me know when you've sighted the *Cary-Anne*."

She spoke hastily and decided on retreat for the moment, tearing down the steps to the cabin below. She paused, gasping for breath, her heart thundering.

What in God's name was she doing? she asked herself.

She was goading him. Because she wanted him to know...

No, that wasn't it. She didn't want to leave him. She loved Virginia, and Patty could take care of business for a few days, and...

She just didn't want to leave him again. Not now. Not after last night. If she let herself be shipped away, awful things could happen. He could be killed; she might never see him again. And even if he could figure out what was happening and survive it, she still might never see him again. Except at Shanna's graduation ceremonies, or at her wedding. And they'd both have escorts, and they'd speak casually and politely...

And it would be as if this thing had never happened between them, as if the full moon hadn't cast its glow upon them and reminded her that she loved him and that there could never be a love such as they shared for her again.

She inhaled sharply.

Was she trying to get him back? She couldn't be doing that; she'd be a fool. There had been so much agony between them in the past.

Her heart slammed hard against her chest.

Maybe it was exactly what she was trying to do. She didn't understand it herself.

## Chapter 5

It was still morning when they reached the waters off the Keys. By ten o'clock, Brent could see the Brennans' beautiful *Cary-Anne* anchored south of Key Largo. His heart quickened with anxiety, but it seemed that everything was all right. No one had gotten to Shanna. Yet.

He pulled as close as he dared and tossed his anchor. He was going to take the dinghy over. Then he saw that the *Cary-Anne* was set with her ladders down and her dive flag up. Maybe he'd jump in and swim over, he was so anxious to see Shanna.

But he paused, remembering Kathy, wondering how he had managed to forget her for a moment. He twisted his jaw, thinking he'd like to hog-tie her at that very moment. What the hell had happened? She'd been so reasonable at first. She couldn't stay— she'd be risking her life. And if anything ever happened to her...

He inhaled and exhaled slowly. If anything ever happened to Kathy, he wouldn't be able to bear it. Time and distance should have made him stronger where she was concerned. But time and distance hadn't done a damned thing.

He'd wanted her more last night than he ever had, more than he'd ever wanted any woman, more than he had wanted life itself. Just as he had known from the first time he'd seen her, when they'd both been little more than kids, that he wanted her, and no one else would ever do.

He'd known he loved her, that he'd always love her. Two people couldn't live as closely and love as intensely for as long as they had and walk away without any emotions remaining. He had believed that the emotions would change, that he could come to care for her in a gentler way.

It hadn't happened.

He closed his eyes and clenched his teeth. It had to happen, because they couldn't go back. Ever. Because he would never forget her miscarriage, the shock that filled them both, then the terror when it had seemed she would never stop bleeding. He remembered the sounds of the sirens clear as day, he remembered pacing the hospital floor and praying as he had never prayed before that she would live. If God didn't want them to have any more children, he didn't give a damn. There were lots of needy children in the world, they could help a few of them. He'd never touch her again, he swore, not in anger, not even in that kind of passion...

Well, he had. Last night. The desire beneath the starlit heaven had been stronger than memory, stronger even, than a vow.

And now they were fighting again, too. Just as they always did. Only it hadn't seemed wrong when they had started out. They were both opinionated, stubborn and determined. They'd had an argument walking down the aisle right after their wedding. With his best man and her maid of honor laughing away, he'd had to lift her and practically throw her into the limousine that took them to their reception. Their anger had dissolved into laughter, then kisses, and he carried her away to their honeymoon suite in his arms. It had always seemed it was all right because they had both known the love was there. And that love had carried them through so very much.

He'd had nothing when they married. He'd made it through Nam, then the G.I. Bill had paid for his college, but little else. He'd had only Kathy and his music. Then they'd had Shanna right away. Those years had been a struggle but they'd weathered them together, both getting through school, while he'd started getting a foothold on his career. When success burst upon them, life became good, and a whirl. They still fought wickedly, made up passionately, yet no matter what, they remained the main core of each other's lives. They'd been so busy, but wherever he went, Kathy usually came along, and Shanna, too. They'd always been a family.

Then they'd had Ryan, and it had seemed that they had everything in life. When they lost Ryan, he'd wondered if they had just had too much. But even then they might have survived. It was just that after this loss, the next baby had meant so very much to Kathy. She'd fallen too quickly into a depression, worrying that the same thing would happen again. She spent hours in the darkness alone.

The doctors had told him he had to shake her out of it. And so he'd snapped at her like a drill sergeant, and he had touched her at last, touched her fury. It had exploded between them and they had argued until he'd dragged her into his arms and into their bed. All the hurt and fury and every other emotion they'd experienced had flared between them, and he had lost control and made love to her fiercely, almost violently. It seemed wonderful right after because she had remained in his arms and they talked again, talked about the new baby, about the future.

But three days later, she had started to scream. And he had burst in upon her to find her in a pool of blood. It hadn't taken long to realize that they hadn't just lost another child. He was about to lose her, and it had been his fault, because of his temper.

He opened his eyes and stared at the sun, shimmering hotly, hovering over him. Dear God, what was he doing to himself? He'd broken out in a cold sweat despite the heat of the day; he was shaking.

"Kathy!" he yelled down to the cabin. "We're here. I'm going over."

He dived into the water and swam with strong strokes for the *Cary-Anne*. He reached the ladder and climbed up, his heart hammering as silence seemed to weigh down upon him.

"Shanna!"

He bellowed his daughter's name, much like an animal in pain. Then he exhaled with relief as he saw her come flying out of the cabin, her blond hair, tied in a ponytail, bouncing behind her. She pitched herself into his arms. "Dad! What are you doing here?"

He hugged her so hard that he felt her squirm beneath his hold, then he released her and framed her face with his hands, trembling inside. "You hadn't heard anything?" he asked her quickly.

She shook her head, her eyes narrowing with concern. David Brennan was on the deck by then, concern written across his features, too. "Mr. McQueen? You're all wet. Where the heck did you come from?" He stopped, confused, then added a hasty, "Sir!"

Brent smiled, wondering if this kid was going to be calling him "Dad" one day. There could be lots of worse things, he thought. David Brennan was a sharp kid with a keen mind who happened to love the water and sports a lot, too.

"I came from the *Sweet Eden*—"

"Mom's boat?" Shanna shrieked. "Oh, I knew it would happen eventually. I just knew it."

"No, no, sweetheart, sorry," he told her softly. "Shanna, David, I've got to talk to you both, and to your parents, David. I've—"

"Where's Mom?" Shanna interrupted anxiously.

He smiled. "I didn't feed her to the sharks, don't worry," he assured her. "I'm sure she'll be over any second now."

"McQueen!" By then David's father, Justin Brennan, had appeared on the deck, a coffee cup in his hand, a broad grin on his face. Brent had hit it off with Justin from the first time they had met, right after their kids had started dating. Justin was a tall, husky guy with white-blond hair and the look of a Viking. He had also served in the army, joined the Dade County police force, been shot up badly, then retired. He'd taken to writing police novels, which had gained a steady following. He had reached a point where he always made the best-seller lists. He'd made a small fortune, remained entirely unpretentious and liked nothing more than a day with his family out on his one new toy—the *Cary-Anne*.

Justin walked across the deck, his hand extended in pleasure. "McQueen, what the hell are you doing here? I'd heard you had some meetings this weekend about a new album."

"Well, those didn't quite come off," Brent explained briefly. Justin's wife, Reba, was coming up the steps. She was a short, cute woman with dark curls, a beautiful smile and lots of ample curves. "More to love," her husband always told her affectionately when she worried about her weight.

"Brent!" she said with pleasure, taking his hand. "We hadn't thought you could make it! How nice to see you. But you're all wet! Where on earth did you come from?"

Brent grinned. Explaining this situation wasn't going to be easy. "There's been some trouble, and I have to take Shanna with me. And yes, Reba, I'm wet, I swam over."

"From where?"

"From Kathy's boat." He started to point to the *Sweet Eden*, but when he turned his voice died and he forgot what he was saying.

Kathy was just coming out of the water. She had decided to swim over, too. And she had dressed for the occasion.

She was wearing a black and teal bikini, a two-piece concoction that seemed to enhance the perfect roundness of her breasts and maybe display just a little too much of them. The bottoms of the suit had those high-cut thighs, and despite her diminutive height, her legs seemed to go on forever beneath them. Her belly was flat and her waist slim, and the little string tie that held the suit together seemed to enhance everything on her body.

He'd liked her naked last night. He'd known then that she was still uncannily perfect and sensual, and he loved the silky feel of her flesh. The suit shouldn't have had any surprises for him, except that . . .

She shouldn't be wearing it. That was it. She shouldn't be that close to naked in front of strangers.

She climbed out of the water, pulling herself up the ladder, a near replica of her teenage daughter. Or Shanna was the replica of her. Something like that.

"Kathy!" Reba seemed even more delighted.

"Mom!"

"Isn't this just wonderful!" Reba said.

Justin was walking over to help Kathy up the ladder. Brent almost brushed past him to do so himself, then managed to control the urge at the last minute. He didn't want anyone else touching her.

It was that damned suit.

She was on the deck, dripping wet, smoothing back her hair, flashing her warm smile at Justin and Reba.

"I can't believe the two of you are here together!" Shanna said.

"We're not," Brent and Kathy said simultaneously. They cast each other a quick glance.

"Did your father get a chance to explain yet?" Kathy asked Shanna anxiously.

There was a pile of towels on a deck chair next to the Brennans' scuba equipment. Brent grabbed a towel and practically threw it over Kathy's shoulders, his fingers taut as he stood behind her, trying very hard to smile and not snarl.

"I haven't had a chance, Kathy. Justin, Reba, I think we'd better sit and I'll try to explain."

A few minutes later they were all in the cabin at the round booth to the starboard side of the very impressive galley. Justin listened in silence, nodding when Brent started with the Harry Robertson case, frowning intently when he heard about Larry's death, then knitting his brows still more tightly when he heard about the explosion. Shanna gasped in horror, realizing that her father should have been there.

"It's all right," Brent assured her gently. It was good to focus on his daughter. Kathy was sitting beside him, and she wouldn't hold on to the towel. It had slipped down her back. And her thigh was touching his. They were all sipping coffee, and her fingers kept brushing his.

He should have hog-tied her and left her on the *Sweet Eden*. He'd be making more sense now.

"I'm all right, and everything is going to be all right," he added, smiling at the anxiety in his daughter's eyes. God, she was precious to him. "But I want you and your mother gone."

"Why?"

He inhaled and exhaled. Damn, but she sounded like her mother!

"Because I don't want you hurt or killed by someone trying very hard to get to me. Shanna, weren't you listening, don't you understand? I tried to disappear the second I saw what had happened to Johnny because I knew I had to get the two of you away before they came looking for me. I did call a friend in Washington and I managed to get everything arranged for the two of you."

"Washington! I don't want to go away. I want to stay near you!"

"Shanna, you can't—"

"You're going to go back! You're going to try to be some kind of bait—"

"Shanna—"

"Wait a minute, wait a minute," Justin interrupted. Brent looked at him. Justin knew he had to go back, that he didn't have a choice in the world.

He also seemed to understand how concerned Brent was for his wife and daughter. *Ex*-wife and daughter.

"What you want is absolute safety for Shanna and Kathy," he said.

"Right," Brent agreed.

"Okay, then listen to this. And you listen real good, young lady," he advised Shanna. "We've got a little place on a private island. Walled in, electric gates, a fine pack of trained shepherds, security guards, the works."

Kathy and Brent were staring at him. Justin flushed, his cheeks going very red. "I have a publisher friend who was in real trouble. Lost his job and everything, and we're always in the islands, so I bought the place from him. The people I've kept on I trust implicitly. I can take care of Shanna and Kathy. We'll still be real near just in case you need us, and Shanna will be a lot happier with David around, and I think Kathy will be happier with us than she would be with strangers, right?"

Brent hesitated. He didn't know what to say. "Justin, I can't put you in this position."

"Hell, Brent, I was a cop for years!"

"But your own family—"

"I'm telling you, this place is like Fort Knox!"

"We'd be delighted to have Kathy and Shanna. Honestly!" Reba said.

David looked at Brent. "Sir, please, we wouldn't have it any other way." He hesitated. "I can't let you take her otherwise, Mr. McQueen."

"Oh, you can't?" Brent said, his temper rising.

"Daddy!" Shanna pleaded. "I won't go unless I go with David."

Brent smiled. She'd been going to fight him the whole way. Then she'd jumped to David's defense, and now she was stuck.

"So you will go with the Brennans."

"You tricked me!" she wailed. "I still don't like this, I don't like it one bit. I want to be with you."

"Shanna," he said, sighing impatiently, "you can't be with me!"

"You could take the boat back and they could be waiting for you."

"I won't take the boat to your mother's place. I'll dock her somewhere else. Shanna, I'll be all right. As long as I'm not worried about you and your mother, I'll be fine."

"Then it's settled!" Justin announced, pleased.

Brent felt Kathy shift beside him. He looked into her eyes, ready for the biggest argument of them all.

"Is it settled?" he asked her tensely.

She smiled. "If this is what you want," she said sweetly.

Her smile was absolutely beautiful, totally innocent. Her eyes were wide and very blue, and her hair was just beginning to dry. It was framing her face with soft, near platinum tendrils.

She was being too agreeable. Maybe she just wanted to get rid of him as soon as possible.

"It's not so much a matter of what I want," he told her. "It's what's necessary."

"All right."

She'd never said "all right" to him in all the years he had known her. Still, he couldn't argue with her because she wasn't arguing with him.

"Maybe we should all start moving," Justin said. He rose. "I want to get these two there as soon as possible."

Brent nodded, rising. He offered Justin his hand. "Thanks."

Justin nodded. "You be careful. Real careful."

"I will be."

He started up the stairs to the deck with the others behind him. "Do you need to get your things?" Reba asked Kathy.

"No, I don't think I need anything at all," Kathy said. Brent narrowed his eyes at her. She smiled at him again. "Really. Shanna and I wear the same size, and I'm sure she has plenty of clothing with her. Do you, Shanna?"

"Of course, Mom," Shanna answered, barely glancing her way. Her eyes were all for her father. "Oh, Dad!" she cried softly, and she threw herself into his arms.

Brent held her long and close, then set her down. "I'll be all right."

She nodded. There were tears in her eyes.

He looked beyond his daughter to his wife. *Ex-*wife. She was standing silently several feet behind Shanna. At long last she'd wrapped the towel around herself. Her eyes met his.

He wanted to sweep her into his arms, to hold her just as he had held his daughter. He couldn't. Not any more. He lifted a hand to her.

"Take care."

She nodded, her blue gaze haunting him. She didn't say a word.

Justin moved to Brent and handed him a card. "This is the name of the guy who used to own the place. The phone and address are still right, in case you want to reach us."

Brent thanked him and stuck the card in his pocket. As soon as he returned to the *Sweet Eden*, he would memorize the numbers and destroy the card. "I'll call from a phone booth and make sure you all got there okay," he said. Shanna was going to start to cry, he thought, if he didn't leave quickly. He kissed her one last time, waved to the others, then felt Kathy's eyes.

She was still staring at him steadily, betraying no emotion whatsoever.

He turned, smiled and dived from the boat into the water.

The second he was gone Kathy dropped her towel and spun her daughter around to face her. "I'm not letting him go back alone, Shanna. I'm going to get on the *Sweet Eden*."

"Kathy, you can't!" Justin protested.

"You can't stop me. And if you waste any more time, you might be risking Shanna." She smiled at him and Reba. "Thank you both so much. For Shanna and for me. Now, I'm awfully sorry, but I have to move fast. He's a stronger swimmer than I am."

She pulled her daughter into her arms and hugged her, then hugged David impulsively while she listened to her daughter's protests.

"Hang around for just a minute, will you?" Kathy asked wryly. "Just in case he has a chance to pull out before I can sneak aboard!"

"I'll stay around," Justin assured her. "I should warn him—"

"Please, don't!" Kathy whispered.

"But, Mother!" Shanna sailed. "Now I'm going to have to worry about both of you."

"Serves you right," Kathy retorted. "Now you'll know how I feel when you ignore the time I tell you to be in at night!"

She couldn't waste any more time. She crawled over the side, not wanting to alert Brent with a splash. She smiled at her daughter. "I love you. We both love you."

"I love you, too!" Shanna cried.

The last sight Kathy had of her daughter then was bittersweet. David stepped up behind her and put a supporting hand around her. They were both very young and very beautiful, and maybe it was just as it should be. There was so much caring between them already.

I'm losing her! Kathy thought, but she wasn't really. Shanna was loving and would always care for her, just as she would always worry about her daughter. But she was going to have to hand her over to David Brennan, it seemed. Maybe much sooner than she had expected.

The water closed around her. Kathy didn't look back. She swam as hard as she could for the *Sweet Eden*.

Brent climbed aboard the *Sweet Eden*, anxious to move as quickly as possible should anyone have tried to follow him and recognized the boat as one belonging to his ex-wife. He wanted to make sure the boat was far, far away from his ex-wife and his daughter.

He was worried. He trusted Justin Brennan, he had a lot of faith in the man, but he would be happier once he placed the call and found they had all reached the island and were behind the gates and walls and protected by the pack of shepherds.

Still, he didn't pull the anchor right away. He took the wet card from his pocket and read the address and phone number, closed his eyes and committed both to memory. Then he ripped the card into tiny shreds and let them fall into the ocean. He walked into the cabin for a towel, then came up and pulled in the anchor.

The *Cary-Anne* had not started out yet. He saw Shanna on deck, watching him, and he waved. She waved in return. David was with her.

He didn't see Kathy anywhere.

He sat, turned the key and listened to the motor rev. Then he slightly angled the tiller and waved again as he headed the *Sweet Eden* toward Miami.

Well, it was over now. Their time together. He didn't have to burn inside and hope he could refrain from grabbing her and demanding to know what the hell she was doing in that bathing suit. He didn't have to worry about the overwhelming desire to touch her, to hold her, to make love to her.

She had very silently, very agreeably stayed behind. She wanted him, she'd had him, and she'd walked away damned easily, ready to resume her life. With Mr. Fashion Plate, Mr. Hair Mousse, Mr. Wall Street Type. Maybe it was just what she wanted, just what she needed. A guy with no passion whatsoever inside, a guy as straight as an arrow...

No passion, no life! He wasn't right for Kathy at all. There was no music in his soul, and Kathy was music, a sweet beat of laughter and impulse and challenge and never-ending curiosity, always willing to take a chance, to travel to new places, to meet new people. She was the pulse, the beat of his life. He hadn't lost his touch when he had lost his son, although the anguish had been terrible. He had lost it all when he had lost her, and he had barely managed to regain it.

Maybe it was better that she dated this guy, this Axel. Maybe they would never walk down island shores together while listening to the drumroll of a different life-style. Maybe they'd never find a private cove and throw caution to the wind. Maybe he'd never make love with sand between his toes.

But then again, maybe he'd never hurt her, either.

She'd walk all over him eventually, Brent thought sourly. Kathy had her own temper. And her own will. And both were powerful. She'd tire of this guy soon enough.

Hell, they were divorced. He should be wishing her happiness. He loved her still, didn't he? He wanted her to be happy. That was what loving was.

Hell, no. He hated Axel, hated the way the guy looked. Hated him touching Kathy.

But then, there wasn't anything he could do about it, was there?

The sun beat down on him as the morning waned to afternoon. He held a course for Bear Cut, determined to drop anchor for a while, then move in at night. He wasn't going to bring the boat in to any dock. He'd drop anchor right off some private property in the grove, then swim in. He'd have the boat picked up by a towing company.

Nightfall was coming. He stood, stretched and stared at the shallow waters before the island. There were still bathers on the darkening beach—lovers, picnickers, kids playing with snorkel gear.

He swung around suddenly, startled, as he heard something. He wasn't sure what it was. Something. Maybe he hadn't heard it. Maybe he'd just sensed it.

Then he did hear something. Below.

Someone had gotten onto the *Sweet Eden*. When he had been with the Brennans?

Or worse, he thought, feeling an unease sweep up his spine. Maybe he'd been so involved with his thoughts that someone had crawled aboard as he'd set out, with him already at the helm.

He was slipping! He'd never stay alive at this rate.

There was a gun in the overhead compartment in the starboard cabin. He'd checked it before, the first chance he'd had last night. Kathy had never moved it. She didn't like guns, but she was a decent shot, and when it had seemed the crime wave across the country was here to stay, he had insisted she do some target practicing with him.

And now someone was in the cabin with his gun.

Well, he still had his hands and his wits and there had been a few too many times in the war when he'd had to use them. It was just that that had been a long time ago.

He moved toward the stairs, then silently moved down them in his bare feet.

There was no one in the galley or in the salon. The intruder had to be in one of the cabins.

He moved to the starboard side. The cabin door was slightly ajar. The shadows had become so deep he could barely see. But then he caught the movement. Someone was in there, moving furtively in the darkness.

He didn't dare make a sound. He catapulted forward, his arms outstretched. The shadow moved then, turning, seeing him.

A scream ripped through the air and the shadow tried to move. An elbow caught him in the chin. His arms wrapped around a warm body and held. Limbs thrashed and flailed as he dragged the body into the hallway, grunting. Then he tackled the body to the ground, straddling it and locking its wrists high above its head.

He blinked against the shadows and darkness. "Kathy!" he exploded.

"Brent!" She was furious, shaking. "You scared me half to death."

"I scared you! I'm supposed to be aboard this boat. You are not!"

"You could have just said that it was you!"

"I thought you were someone trying to kill me," he told her.

"Well, that just might be true at this moment! Why didn't you say—"

"I try not to announce my presence when I think someone might have a gun," he drawled wryly.

"You didn't have to manhandle me! Now get off me!" she snapped, her blue eyes flashing with fury.

He was about to do so, but then he shook his head with a grim smile and sat, still holding her wrist, still straddling her hips, his weight settled comfortably on his haunches.

"I don't think so."

"What?"

He leaned toward her. "Not until you tell me what the hell you think you're doing on this boat!"

## Chapter 6

I'm going with you," Kathy said.

"What?"

She inhaled and exhaled, feeling the pressure of his hands and thighs upon her. She could see an angry tic at the base of his throat. "I'm going with you," she repeated.

He exploded with a swift, precise oath.

"Will you please quit that and listen to me for a moment? And while you're at it, would you please let go of me? This is not the most comfortable position in the world."

"It seems to be the only position to have you in, Ms. O'Hara, to know where you are and what you're doing!"

"Brent!"

He got up and none-too-gently and very ungraciously dragged her to her feet. He stared at her in the growing darkness, turned and climbed the stairs. Kathy quickly followed.

"Brent, will you listen to me?"

He was standing there, his hands on his hips, staring out at the beach. In the coming darkness, the place was almost deserted. All the children had returned to their various boats with their parents and were heading to the marinas. The picnickers were all gone. A lone couple walked the sands hand in hand.

"Kathy, I'm putting you on a plane out of here," he told her flatly.

"No, you're not!" she retorted furiously. "Do you want to know what the problem is, Brent? I know what you're trying to do. You don't want to go home and play it safe. You want to go back and make sure you're incredibly visible. You want to draw this person or these persons out."

He turned to stare at her. Even in the darkness she was certain she could see a glitter in his eyes. She had hit upon the truth. "Kathy—"

"I'm right and I know it!" she said stubbornly.

"Kathy! I don't know what I'm doing, and I don't know just how good these people are. I—"

"My house is probably the safest place in Miami for you, Brent. Had you thought of that?"

The moonlight was growing stronger, cutting through the shadows of the night. He inclined his head, watching her with a certain amusement. 'Is it?''

"Yes, it is. And don't laugh at me. I know what I'm talking about."

"*Our* house, remember? And if it's so safe, why was I able to walk right into the bathroom?"

"Because you know about that entrance. Because I hadn't bothered with the alarm because I knew Sam was out there. No one gets past Sam."

"I did."

"Because I never managed to explain the terms of the divorce to him!" Kathy snapped. "Brent, that foolish dog loves you. But he's wonderful otherwise. And the alarm system is connected directly to the police station. And we can even bring in a cop or a security guard or—"

"Kathy, don't you understand? You would be safest if you were far away," he said with exasperation.

She was silent for a moment. "No. I can't go away. Don't you understand?"

They both felt the rocking of the boat, the gentle movement of the waves, the coolness of the night breeze. He stared at her then sank on to the bench, sighing. "Kathy, I wasn't going to even bring the boat into her berth. I was going to ditch her somewhere close and—"

"I know the perfect place!" Kathy said enthusiastically. "Mrs. Fenniman's property."

"Whose?"

"Mrs. Fenniman's! She lives at the little curve in the arm of the peninsula. She's ninety-something years old, lives with a sweet young nurse and has the most overgrown acre of land I've ever seen. And you can run along the back of it and right up the side of our wall to the gate and be inside the house before anyone could possibly know you'd been outside it!"

He watched her for a long moment, knowing she was absolutely right.

Then suddenly the moon touched his eyes and Kathy saw that they were flashing with fury again. He stood and walked over to her and caught her shoulders and seemed to be fighting the temptation to shake her hard.

"Why are you doing this?" he demanded harshly.

She let her head fall back and met his gaze with an equal fury and challenge. "For old time's sake," she snapped.

"Kathy—"

"Because I don't want to be forced out of my own house, all right? What difference does it make? You cannot force me to go anywhere, Brent!"

"Don't bet on it. I thought earlier that I should have tied you up and sent you north in a cargo box."

She wrenched back from his touch, taking a step away from him. "I'd never speak to you again."

# SILHOUETTE®

## ♥ PRESENTS ♥

# *A Real Sweetheart of a Deal!*

6
FREE
GIFTS

**PEEL BACK THIS CARD AND SEE WHAT YOU CAN GET! THEN...**

## *Complete the Hand Inside* ➤

It's easy! To play your cards right, just match this card with the cards inside.

Turn over for more details...

## *Incredible, isn't it? Deal yourself in right now and get 6 fabulous gifts* **ABSOLUTELY FREE.**

### 1. 4 BRAND NEW SILHOUETTE INTIMATE MOMENTS® NOVELS—FREE!

Sit back and enjoy the excitement, romance and thrills of four fantastic novels. You'll receive them as part of this winning streak!

### 2. A LOVELY GOLD-PLATED CHAIN—

**FREE!** You'll love your elegant 20k gold electroplated chain! The necklace is finely crafted with 160 double-soldered links and it's electroplate finished in genuine 20k gold. And it's yours free as added thanks for giving our Reader Service a try!

### 3. AN EXCITING MYSTERY BONUS—FREE!

And still your luck holds! You'll also receive a special mystery bonus. You'll be thrilled with this surprise gift. It is useful as well as practical.

## *PLUS*

### THERE'S MORE. THE DECK IS STACKED IN YOUR FAVOR. HERE ARE THREE MORE WINNING POINTS. YOU'LL ALSO RECEIVE:

### 4. FREE HOME DELIVERY

Imagine how you'll enjoy having the chance to preview the romantic adventures of our Silhouette heroines in the convenience of your own home! Here's how it works. Every month we'll deliver 4 new Silhouette Intimate Moments® novels right to your door. There's no obligation to buy, and if you decide to keep them, they'll be yours for only $2.74* each—that's a saving of 21¢ per book! And there's no charge for postage and handling — there are no hidden extras!

### 5. A MONTHLY NEWSLETTER—FREE!

It's our special *"Silhouette" Newsletter* your privileged look at upcoming books and profiles of our most popular authors.

### 6. MORE GIFTS FROM TIME TO TIME—FREE!

It's easy to see why you have the winning hand. In addition to all the other special deals available only to our home subscribers, when you join the Silhouette Reader Service™, you can look forward to additional free gifts throughout the year.

## *SO DEAL YOURSELF IN – YOU CAN'T HELP BUT WIN!*

**Remember!** To win this hand, all you have to do is place your
sticker inside and DETACH AND MAIL THE CARD BELOW.
You'll get four free books, a free gold-plated chain and a
mystery bonus.

### BUT DON'T DELAY!
### MAIL US YOUR LUCKY CARD TODAY!

If card is missing write to:
Silhouette Reader Service, 901 Fuhrmann Blvd., P.O. Box 1867, Buffalo, NY 14269-1867

---

## BUSINESS REPLY CARD

First Class    Permit No. 717    Buffalo, NY

Postage will be paid by addressee

SILHOUETTE READER SERVICE™
901 Fuhrmann Blvd.
P.O. Box 1867
Buffalo, N.Y.
14240-9952

NO POSTAGE
NECESSARY
IF MAILED
IN THE
UNITED STATES

"Well, you haven't spoken to me in three years."

"I'll have you nice and safe in jail on charges of physical harassment or whatever it is you call it!" she warned him.

He laughed and before she knew it had caught her by the shoulders again, swung her around and set her on the bench by the tiller, then stood towering over her, locking her in place with a hand laid flat upon the fiberglass next to each shoulder.

"This is my party you've crashed, Kathy. And things are going to be done my way."

"I beg your pardon! You crashed into my bathroom, remember?"

"*Our* bathroom!"

"Brent—"

"It's almost like you're inviting me to play man and wife again. Is that what you're doing, Kathy?"

"Get off me, Brent. I'm trying to help you. For Shanna's sake. For—"

"For old time's sake. Yes, I know." He straightened suddenly and walked away from her. He stared at the water, then said, "All right. All right, you can stay, but we still play it my way. I make all the rules. Agreed?"

"No, you do not—"

"Kathy, trust me, I wouldn't feel a bit guilty exercising a little physical harassment to get you to safety."

"What are these rules?" she demanded. Muttering beneath her breath, she added, "I don't believe this! I've done my very best to be an extremely decent ex-wife, and here you are—"

"Making rules. Right. That's the way it goes. Agreed?"

"I told you—let me hear the rules."

"Once we get to the house, you stay in it. You don't even walk to the pool unless I'm with you, understand? You don't bring in the mail. You don't do anything."

"Brent—"

"Anything at all. All right?"

She clenched her teeth and nodded. "All right!"

"And," he added softly, "if you want to play house, Ms. O'Hara, we play house."

"What?" she said.

"I'm not sleeping on any couches. Or in Shanna's room or on the floor."

Warmth sizzled through her. She knew what he was saying. It was just that her tongue had gone very dry and she wasn't at all sure of how she should respond.

"I—I don't mind couches or Shanna's room," she said softly.

"That's not what I meant and you know it. I can't live with you and not sleep with you. You're not my wife, but you were for a very long time, and I discovered years ago that I didn't seem to be able to manage any halfway situations with you. If you want me in the house, you get me in your bed. Understood?''

She stared at him blankly and wondered if he had just given her exactly what she wanted. Or if he had frightened her beyond anything she had expected.

What had she wanted? Flowers? Soft music? A careful seduction? Maybe she was pretending. And maybe she had wanted him to play the game, too. Perhaps there was no getting back together, ever, because the desire they shared blanketed the pain, but in the harsh light of day, it could never erase it.

''Kathy!'' His voice was curt, nearly brutal, and cold as ice.

''I'm thinking!'' she snapped.

''You didn't have to think so long last night,'' he reminded her bluntly. ''Last night you were just about as hot as—''

''You bastard!'' she gasped, leaping to her feet and staring at him furiously, her fingers curling into fists at her sides. They wouldn't stay there. She took a step forward and slammed them against his naked chest. He caught her wrists and dragged her hard against him, his eyes sizzling as they bored into hers.

''I'm just trying to keep this blunt and true and in perspective, Ms. O'Hara. I told you before I won't play games. I wouldn't pretend that what happened between us didn't. And I won't turn anything into a game, either. I won't bed down on a couch then come wandering around in the middle of night pretending I'm looking for something I can't find. You wanted me last night, I wanted you. I still want you. And if I'm going to sleep in that house, I'm damned well going to sleep with you.''

She couldn't stare at him much longer. Maybe he was right, maybe it should all be kept strictly on the surface. It would be foolish to pretend, even to herself, that she didn't want him desperately. Even if it was just for this brief time.

It had been his house, too. Technically, it still was. Maybe he couldn't live in it and keep his distance. She knew Brent well; he wasn't going to date her at this time in their lives.

She wished he hadn't been quite so blunt, but he meant to be. Blunt, crude, basic. He didn't want her to expect more out of him.

She wrenched from his hold. ''All right.''

He arched a brow. ''You agree?''

''I just said so.''

He smiled slowly. She tossed her blond hair, turned and started for the steps.

''Where are you going now?'' he demanded harshly.

She had reached the stairs. She swung around, angry. ''You've got a bit of a ride to the shore. I'm going to bed. Alone. We haven't reached the house yet!''

She started down the steps, infuriated. She heard his soft laughter follow her, and it didn't help one bit. She slammed her cabin door and flung herself on the bed, her heart racing. She waited tensely, wondering if he would come after her with some new ultimatum.

But he didn't. She heard the motor rev, felt the motion of the boat, and she knew they were under way. He hadn't come near her.

He didn't need to, she reminded herself. He already had her exactly where he wanted her. All he had to do was bide his time.

She hadn't thought she would doze off, but she'd probably had less than four hours of sleep the night before and, to her amazement, once she closed her eyes, the rocking of the boat allowed the world to slip away.

She was startled when she heard Brent's voice awakening her. "Kathy! Kathy, we're here."

She sat up and saw his silhouette in the doorway. She blinked, trying to leave the fog of sleep behind her. It was so dark. They hadn't come into a marina.

No, no, they weren't supposed to be at a marina. They were on the shore of Mrs. Fenniman's property. It had been her idea. Whatever had possessed her?

Despite the moon, it was still very black out. And there was no nice clean beach here, just weeds and high grass and all kinds of trees and yucky underwater plants.

"Come on!" Brent urged her. Even in the shadows, she felt his eyes wander over her. She was still dressed in the bikini—Shanna's bikini—and nothing else. Well, it was appropriate for a swim.

"Have you got your sneakers and the keys?"

"Sneakers?"

"Yeah, you never know what you might step on trying to get out of here."

"Oh, yeah, right!" she agreed miserably. She found her sneakers beneath the bunk and tied them on. Then she dug into her bag to find her keys and wallet. Brent reached for them and she stared at him blankly. "I've got pockets," he told her curtly. "You've barely got room to breathe."

After handing him her things, she waltzed past him and hurried up on deck.

There wasn't a soul around, not for miles and miles. Brent had turned off all the lights and brought them in to hug the shore. The tide might ground them by morning, but that didn't seem to matter much right now.

"Ready?" he asked her.

If only it had been a nice clean beach.

"Sure," she murmured. She didn't want to dive into the water. They were close enough to the marina for the water to be filled with oil and garbage. They were far enough away for it to be filled with all kinds of creatures she didn't mind at all by daylight—but hated in the darkness.

"Let's go."

She must have hesitated too long. He swept her up and tossed her over, then followed quickly.

She was a good swimmer. She clenched her teeth and headed in, trying to ignore the muddy sand and slimy feel of the sea grasses. She stumbled for a foothold when she neared land. She almost slipped in the stuff but Brent was right behind her, taking her elbow. They walked to the hard earth together. Then he had her hand and was leading her silently through the sea brush, through the stands of mangroves and deep into the foliage of the yard.

She could see Mrs. Fenniman's old Spanish mansion up on a rise. They came to the row of pines at the base of the ledge and ran along them until they reached the back wall of their fence.

"Don't bark, Sam! Don't bark!" Brent muttered.

He paused just a second, then led her to the front of the property. He glanced quickly at Kathy as he looked at the alarm box.

"I haven't changed the code," she muttered.

He punched in the numbers, then opened the wrought-iron gate with her key. He shoved her inside and followed quickly, locking it behind him.

Kathy nearly screamed as something cold touched her hand. She jumped a mile before she realized it was Sam.

"Good dog!" Brent said, patting him affectionately. "Come on," he told Kathy.

They hurried up the path to the door, which Brent opened. Sam started to follow them in. "All right, just for a few minutes," Brent told the dog. "We need you out there tonight, my friend."

Kathy sighed and leaned against the door for a moment, then moved away as Brent continued to pat Sam. "Where are you going?" he demanded sharply.

"For a glass of wine. And then I'm going to take a bath. Every creepy thing in the sea seemed to have touched me."

"Wait a minute," he told her curtly.

She stood and watched him while he disappeared into her bedroom.

*Their* bedroom.

He came back a moment later. She stared at him curiously. "I was just checking the back door."

She smiled sweetly. "The riffraff has already come in that way."

He ignored her and picked up the phone. She walked into the kitchen and poured herself a glass of wine, then decided to be generous and pour him a glass, too.

When she emerged from the kitchen, he seemed to be on hold. The receiver was between his head and his shoulder and he was busy loading a gun.

"Where did that come from?"

He glanced at her, arching a brow. "It's a police gun, fires fifteen shots."

She shivered despite herself. There was a gun on the boat; he'd always kept a gun in the house. This was a new one, though.

"Robert gave it to me a while back. I have a permit, and it's nice and legal." She was still staring at him. "Kathy, if someone comes in and tries to shoot us, I'm going to shoot back. Okay?"

"You brought that off the boat?"

"I brought it with me the other day, when I came in through the bathroom."

Just how long had he been in the house before she had seen him? she wondered. Not that it mattered any more. She set down his glass of wine.

He cast her a quick glance. "Thanks."

"Sure."

"Robert? Yeah, it's Brent," he said suddenly into the phone. He had called Robert; he was bringing the police in on the situation.

She could hear Robert's voice, demanding to know where he was, where he'd been. "Robert, hang on just a second," he said as Kathy started to turn away. "You're taking a bath?"

She nodded, wondering if he thought she was giving him some kind of an invitation. She wasn't—she felt dirty from swimming in dirty water.

"Good," he said bluntly. "Burn that suit when you're done, will you?"

She arched a brow in surprise, but he had already turned his attention to the phone conversation. She walked into the bathroom with her wine, turned on the water in the tub, poured in an ample amount of bubbles, then lowered herself into it.

The heat was delicious. The clean water was delicious. She sank beneath the water, soaked her hair and scrubbed it assiduously. She leaned back, content, and took a long swallow of wine.

Was this an invitation?

It hadn't been that long ago when she had lain here dreaming of the past. Then the past had intruded upon the present. She had thought about Brent crawling into the tub with her. And he had stumbled into it, jeans and all. Not exactly what she'd had in mind.

None of this was what she'd had in mind....

Would he come in now? she wondered. Come in now as she had dreamed, stride in, peel away the cutoffs, sink down with her. Touch her in the midst of the bubbles, do the things to her he done the night before...

Her eyes closed. He would come, he was the one who insisted he would. He would sweep her up as he had so often before, and lay her on the bed they had shared. Against the whiteness of the cool, clean cotton sheets. His body would look so bronze.

It would be like playing house all over again. Playing man and wife as Brent had said.

They could never go back. But that was all right. She only wanted these few nights. . . .

Brent came in, talking. "I'll see Robert tomorrow," he said. "They'll have a man watching the house tonight. They had a patrol car going around when we came in, but apparently the man didn't see us. I don't know if that means we're very good, or he isn't quite so good. But between the alarm and the dog and the cop, I guess we should be in pretty good shape."

She didn't respond. Her head was on the rim of the tub, her eyes were closed, her dark honey lashes sweeping her cheeks. He smiled suddenly, realizing she was sound asleep.

"You can drown yourself that way," he whispered softly. He pulled a towel from the rack and bent to lift her. Her eyes flew open with alarm.

"It's all right, don't be frightened. It's just me. You were sleeping."

Her eyes fluttered, and her arms wound around his neck. He thought she had fallen asleep again already when she whispered softly, "Just you, don't be frightened!" she said. "I should be absolutely terrified."

"Why is that?"

She shook her head. Her eyes closed.

He carried her to the bedroom, pulled back the spread, then laid her on the sheets, still wrapped in the towel. He rolled her, freeing the towel from beneath her. She lay on her stomach. Her eyes opened and closed again.

Her back was still damp. He moved the terry-cloth towel gently over her, then tossed it aside. He pressed his lips against her spine and felt her slight shift of movement. She tried to open her eyes but her lashes fell softly over them once again.

He smiled, rose and brought the covers over her, then turned off the light as he left the room.

In the living room he sat before the fireplace and drank his wine. Sam pushed his nose onto Brent's lap and Brent idly patted the dog. "You don't understand any of it, do you, boy? Neither do I," Brent assured him.

He leaned back. He shouldn't be here. He shouldn't have let her talk him into anything. He should have put her on a plane.

But it was good to be here. With her.

"She came back for me, Sam. I left her on a sailboat, heading away with friends, and she came back. What do you think of that? Actually, it was pretty humiliating. Here I am thinking I can still hear a pin drop in the dark, and she crawled right on that boat without my even realizing it. I'm slipping, Sam. Her

fault. I was thinking about her. I haven't been able
to stop thinking about her for a minute."

He stroked the dog's ears a few minutes longer,
then sighed and rose. "Out, Sam. I need you outside. To watch for bad guys. Don't let me down,
boy."

With Sam out, Brent finished his wine. He was
feeling the slime himself, and chose to shower in the
hallway bathroom rather than take a chance on
waking her up.

The heat and the steam felt great. He came out
with a towel wrapped around his hips and made one
last tour of the place. Robert had already made sure
the alarm was working, and the cop was outside
somewhere. And he did have a lot of faith in Sam.

He picked up the gun and carried it with him into
the bedroom. The lights were always left on in the
pool area, and he could see from the bathroom window that nothing seemed to be disturbing the peace
of the yard.

Satisfied, he started for the bedroom. Then he saw
her bikini on the floor.

He sniffed, bent to pick it up and tossed it into the
trash can. Then he flicked off the bathroom light and
silently walked into the bedroom. He slipped the gun
beneath his pillow, discarded the towel and crawled
in beside her.

He had no intention of waking her. He lay in the comfort of the bed, tired but not sleeping, feeling the luxury of the sheets after the night on the hard deck.

Then she started to move toward him. He turned. She came even closer.

He slipped an arm around her. He smelled the sweet scent of her shampoo in her still damp hair, and the delicate, subtle scent of the perfumed soap she used. He wasn't going to wake her. . . .

He stroked the softness of her upper arms. Her back fit provocatively against his chest, and her derriere was right up against a rapidly hardening part of his anatomy. He needed to push her away just a bit.

He set his palm upon her hip, but he didn't quite manage to push. Instead his palms tenderly cupped the curve, then stroked the rounded fullness there with a sensual appreciation. He heard her moan softly. She was still half asleep. . . . But she was also half awake.

He swept his hand from her hip to her breast. Slowly, he caressed the lushness of her flesh, the tempting hardness of the bud of her nipple. She moved slightly, adjusting her body more tightly against his. He swept his hand over her belly and laid his lips against the nape of her neck, then her earlobe, all the while moving his hands upon her.

He tossed the sheet aside and saw the gleam of her naked flesh in the night glow that touched the room. He groaned.

He stroked the rise of her hips once again, pushed her thigh forward, then thrust himself fully and deeply within her from behind. He heard the sharp intake of her breath and pulled her closer against him. Her scent was sweetly intoxicating. The movement of her body was subtle yet wildly erotic. He kept running his hands over her naked hips and buttocks, then slipped them to her belly, bringing her nearer to meet the force of his thrust. He lost all sense of finesse and thundered against her. The climax rose within him unbearably, his body constricted with the need, with the desire, with the pleasure and the anguish, then seemed to erupt. Shudder after shudder went through him, and he thrust and thrust until he was emptied within her. He heard her cry out softly, and even as he drifted down, he pulled her to him again, loathe to pull away. He stayed within her, just holding her gently.

She didn't speak, but she seemed content.

He smoothed her hair from beneath his nose. In time, he dozed.

Kathy awoke with a start when his hand landed with a not really gentle crack on her rear. She started up, sweeping the sheets around her and staring at him with daggers and reproach.

"What was that for?"

"You have to get up."

"You didn't have to slap me!"

"That was just a love tap," he said with a wave of his hand. He had been up for a while, she surmised. He was dressed in jeans and a red polo shirt. He had shaved and seemed in top form.

While she felt ancient, exhausted. She hadn't a speck of makeup on, and her hair was probably one big tangle.

"Rough night?" he asked her. "I didn't mean to wake you."

He seemed so damned cocky. She couldn't resist. "You didn't!" she told him innocently.

He cast her a warning, reproachful glare and pretended for a moment that he would get her with the towel he had just plucked from the floor. She had to laugh, and he smiled and turned away. Her laughter faded because she knew that once he would have tossed himself over her, warned her that he was going to be damned sure she was awake this time, and made love to her all over again.

But this wasn't the past, and he was only here because all their lives might be in danger.

"Robert is on his way over," he told her. "Coffee's on. I thought you could make the omelets this time. And they'd better be good. I'm starving. Some first mate you turned out to be. I didn't get a thing to eat all day."

She arched a brow, sitting up, pulling the sheets to her chest. "I don't remember inviting you to any meals."

She groaned and turned to the refrigerator for the butter. He was behind her, taking the knife from her hand, spinning her around in his arms. He was frowning, perplexed.

"What is the matter?"

"Nothing."

"Kathy."

"Nothing, really. I—" Her eyes fell. "I just wish you wouldn't play that song."

His eyes softened instantly. He smiled, and it was a curious smile, filled with tenderness and with pain. "I know. It seems to embody years, doesn't it? Our entire youth."

No, our love! she wanted to say. But she didn't. She had already said too much.

"It just . . . hurts," she said.

He pulled her against him, cradling her very tenderly. And they seemed to stand there forever. She felt his touch as she hadn't felt it before. She felt the tenderness and the magic that had always been there. She felt the elusive bond that had held them so tightly for so long. She felt the love, all the years they had shared, everything that had ever been right and natural.

Then the knife slipped and fell to the floor with a clang and they stepped quickly away from each other. Kathy turned quickly toward the refrigerator and Brent moved around the counter.

"I was thinking about the tour," he told her, "because Harry Robertson always seemed to be humming that tune. Nervously. And then sometimes I would catch him whistling it, and when I would look at him, he would always break off."

"Maybe he was afraid you'd think he was trying to steal your song," Kathy said.

Brent shook his head. "No, no, it wasn't anything like that. It was more like he absolutely hated the song."

"He couldn't have. No one hates that song. It's one of the most beautiful you've ever written. It hit the charts for months on end! It's almost twenty years old and little kids and teenagers still seem to know it."

"Well, Harry Robertson hated it," Brent said flatly.

Kathy beat the eggs and said curtly, "Want to do the toast, please?"

"Sure. We have to keep your strength up, too," he told her idly.

Then they both stopped because they heard Sam barking like crazy.

"Get down!" Brent snapped to Kathy. She saw that the gun was in his hand. He had been wearing it the whole time they had been talking.

"Brent—"

"Get on the floor, Kathy!"

He was heading toward the front door, wary, silent, alert. He leaned against the door frame and carefully stared out the peephole. He started to laugh.

"Brent, have you lost your mind?" Kathy demanded.

He turned to her, smiling. "No, just my instincts, I think. I guess you'd better throw on a few more eggs. It's just Robert. He's at the gate looking sadly perplexed. Poor Robert! Sam never did seem to take to him."

Brent grinned and opened the door to step out. Sighing with relief, Kathy reached for another egg. Then she heard the gunshot. For a single instant she froze with terror.

Then she screamed and raced for the door.

## Chapter 7

Common sense didn't enter Kathy's thinking. She had heard the crack, and had horrified visions of Brent lying face down in a pool of blood.

She didn't pause at the door; she didn't look through the peephole. She threw open the door, screaming his name. Then she pelted down the walkway with such speed that she flew into him as he stood before the gate. The two of them tumbled to the ground together.

"Brent!"

There was nothing on him, no blood, no injury. His eyes weren't closed in pain. Instead they were wide open, staring into hers as if she was danger-

ously insane. She was on top of him, then Sam was
on them both, licking Brent's face.

"Sam, quit!" Brent insisted. "Kathy, what the hell
is the matter with you?"

"The shot! I heard a shot!"

"You heard a shot so you came running out the
door? You idiot! If there had been a shot, you should
have stayed the hell inside!"

He wasn't injured, he wasn't even touched, and
according to him, there hadn't even been a shot. But
she'd heard it! She was here because of her fear for
him.

Her eyes narrowed. "Fine! The next time I think
you might be in trouble, I'll let you bleed to death!"

"It would be smarter than running out here to
bleed to death along with me!" he swore.

"Children, children, children!"

Kathy realized that a pair of feet shod in black
moccasins was planted by their side. She looked up
slowly to find that Robert McGregor had come in
through the gate while the two of them sat entwined, arguing. "Getting along the same as usual,
I see."

"Kathy, get off me," Brent groaned.

"Oh, Kathy, get off me yourself!" she spat out.
"You never oblige when I ask you to get off me."

"Ah, the plot thickens," Robert commented.

Kathy flushed. How could she have said what she
said with Robert standing right there? It was Brent's

fault; he was always goading her, it seemed. Whether he meant to or not.

Brent rose, then with hands planted firmly on her waist, he helped her up. She smiled sweetly at Robert. "The plot isn't doing a darn thing, Lieutenant McGregor, I assure you."

"Oh, I think it's wonderfully thick," Brent muttered darkly. "Kathy was going to save me from bullets with a shield of human flesh. Great idea, huh?"

"Bullets!" Robert said, then smiled at Kathy. "Kath, no bullets. An old car going down the street backfired, that was all."

She smiled over clenched teeth. "Wonderful."

"Maybe we shouldn't be standing here like this, though," Robert said. "Not that I think that anything is going to happen here. Let's go inside."

Kathy led the way in. Robert followed Brent. She ignored them both and went into the kitchen. She heard Brent telling Robert about Shanna, then she heard him go into an explanation of everything he had known or suspected when Harry Robertson had been arrested.

"You're sure that that's what's going on?" Robert asked him.

Kathy picked up an egg as she watched Brent shrug. "What else? Why, do you think—"

"I think what you think," Robert said. "It's just we've got no leads, no clues. The bombing that killed

Johnny was a very professional job. Whoever did it knew exactly what he was doing. And I'm sure you weren't meant to be in the explosion. I think someone thinks you know something."

"Well, I don't," Brent assured him. "I don't know a damned thing."

Kathy added another egg to her mixture, watching the two men intently. She knew Brent well enough to believe his exasperated statement.

Robert ran his fingers through his short, dark hair. "What are you going to do about the benefit Friday night?"

Kathy reached into a cabinet beneath the counter for a frying pan. She set it on the counter.

"Robert—" Brent warned.

"What benefit?" Kathy demanded, leaning over the counter to challenge them both, pan in hand.

Robert arched a brow to Brent and looked at Kathy uneasily. "Kathy, it's been in the paper—"

"What benefit?" she repeated.

"It's not a concert or anything. Just a big party out on Star Island. To raise money for the homeless," Brent told her.

"Well, you can't do it," Kathy said. "Obviously. Robert, tell him he can't do it. It would be idiotic."

"Kathy, I'm doing the damned benefit," Brent stated irritably.

"Robert, tell him—"

"I think he might need to do it more than ever now, Kathy."

"Don't you see, Kath? It might be the only way to talk to people involved, to try to figure out—"

"Are you both crazy?" Kathy exploded. "Brent, you wanted me out of town. You didn't think that my house was safe! Now you want to go out to somebody else's place and be surrounded by all those people—"

"People I've worked with," Brent reminded her.

She stared at them incredulously. They thought Brent should go.

"Robert!" she wailed furiously. "How can you let him do this?"

"Kathy, we've got nothing! And he's not going to stay in a closet for the rest of his life, you know that! The place will be crawling with police and security."

"It will probably be the safest place in the world for me to be," Brent assured her.

"You're not a detective!" Kathy exploded.

She watched the stubborn set of his jaw and his voice went low, which tended to mean he was very angry. "Kathy, I need to go. What the hell are you doing with those eggs? Aren't they ready yet?"

"What?" she snapped.

"I said, what about—"

"The eggs, yes, well, they're right here, you all enjoy them!" She strode out of the kitchen, the frying pan still in her hand. Frightened and infuriated, she thrust it at Brent, catching him soundly in the stomach with it. She heard him grunt as she hurried down the hallway to her room.

Brent held the pan, gritting his teeth around the pain. Then he smiled at Robert. "She really loves me, you can tell," he said.

Robert laughed, then sobered quickly. "I can give you a lot of protection but no guarantees, Brent. Do you really think doing the benefit is such a good idea? Maybe you should just disappear for a while."

Brent shook his head. "What am I going to do, Robert, run for the rest of my life? I have to try to find out what this is all about."

He walked around the counter into the kitchen with the frying pan. "Eggs?" he asked.

Robert winced. "I think I'll just take some coffee."

"Oh, come on. My omelets are better than hers anyway."

"Maybe she'll join us in time, huh?" Robert said.

"Oh, I don't know. She has a heck of a temper."

"Well, so do you."

Brent lowered his head. "I know that. Yeah, hell, I know that!" he replied wearily.

"She came running out of the house like that because she was concerned."

"I know that, too. It's just she scared the damn hell out of me, that's all. Hey, Robert, get out of my personal life and be useful, won't you? Throw in some toast."

Brent finished the omelets. As the two of them ate, Robert went over every little thing one more time and Brent answered as slowly and carefully as he could.

Brent gave Robert the number where he could reach the Brennans, explaining that he didn't want to call from the house in case there was some kind of a tap on the phone. Robert promised to make sure that Shanna and everyone else had arrived safely on the island.

Then Robert went to the door to leave. "I've people up at the state prison, trying to find out what they can from any of the inmates who were associated with Harry Robertson. Maybe we'll come up with something from that angle. I've talked to Keith Montgomery, and I've talked to the Hicks brothers. They don't seem to know anything, either. I've got twenty-four-hour security going for them, too. Maybe you should talk among yourselves."

"I was planning to do just that, at the benefit."

"They're going to bury Johnny this afternoon," Robert said.

Brent glanced toward the bedroom. "Yeah, I know, I picked it up on the news."

"You were planning on going?"

"Yeah, I didn't want to say anything. Hey, Johnny was a real pill sometimes. We didn't often see eye to eye, and we didn't get along that great. But I worked with him enough over the years. I wouldn't feel right if I didn't go.''

··''What!'' came a sharp exclamation. Brent spun around. Kathy was out of the bedroom. ''Now you're going to go running around to funerals, too!''

''Kathy, I have to go.''

''Then I'm going.''

''The hell you are!''

''Hey, hey, hey!'' Robert protested. ''Kathy, listen to this. Brent, you listen, too. I'll come for you both in time for the services, all right?''

''She shouldn't—'' Brent began.

''*I* shouldn't! What about you?''

''You're starting to sound married again,'' Robert warned them.

It worked. They fell silent. Robert smiled and waved. ''The funeral could be interesting, too, you know,'' he told Brent.

Kathy turned to go to the bedroom. Brent saw Robert out. He paused by his car, looking at the house. ''This is a good setup here. The gate, the fence, the dog, the fact that the peninsula is private and a getaway would be almost impossible. No one's coming after you here, not even a professional. It couldn't be a clean enough job.''

''Thanks,'' Brent said wryly.

''Seriously—''

''I know.''

''I'll be back.''

Inside Brent picked up the dishes. Kathy hadn't come out to eat. Almost two hours later she still hadn't appeared.

Brent watched the news, then sat at the piano. He picked out notes and played rhythms and beats, until his fingers started to move over the keys to "Forever My Love." Then he hesitated, remembering she hadn't wanted to hear the song.

Brent closed his eyes, thinking. There had been something about Harry and that song....

He opened his eyes. Kathy was standing there in a handsome navy business suit, her hair pulled back and wound into an elegant knot at her nape. "Are you going like that?" she asked him, indicating his jeans.

He smiled. "That depends. I was waiting to crawl through the closet. What have I got to wear?"

She shrugged. "I don't remember. But you've waited pretty long. Robert should be back soon."

"I didn't wait on purpose. You were in the bedroom."

"I don't remember that stopping you from entering before," she said flatly.

His smile deepened. "I'll remember that," he told her.

She turned on her navy heels, leaving him at the piano. She was cold, very cold. Like ice. Anything he might have gained in their time together, he had now lost, he thought.

He left the piano, entered the bedroom and rummaged through the huge closet until he found a suit. By the time he had changed, Kathy was calling through the door that Robert had come.

When Brent came out, Kathy told him Robert had checked on Shanna and that their daughter was fine and safe and sent her love.

Brent nodded and thanked Robert.

They rode to the church in the police car. The church was filled to overflowing, and the curious and the fans spilled into the streets. Teenagers carried banners proclaiming, "We'll love you forever, Johnny Blondell!"

Services were brief, then they moved on to the cemetery. Brent spoke with Johnny's sister, who had made the arrangements and seemed to be the one person there who had really loved Johnny Blondell.

He looked around while the priest's words droned on at the grave site. Kathy stood at his side; Marla Harrington, sniffing into a handkerchief, stood not far away. Cops surrounded the area.

Keith Montgomery didn't make a showing; neither did either of the Hicks brothers.

When the service ended Brent felt a tap on his arm. Then he was suddenly engulfed in a massive and emotional hug as Marla threw her arms around him. She kissed his cheek and held him tight and looked at him with her huge velvet-brown eyes. "Oh, Brent! Poor Johnny, how horrible. And I was so, so worried about you! I called and called, and I drove by the house, and I talked to Keith and the others and no one, absolutely no one, not your manager, not your press secretary, no one knew where you were or how you were!''

He disentangled himself carefully from her arms. ''I've been fine, Marla, fine. And I've hardly been gone a long time.''

''It's just that I wanted to be with you so badly when I heard!'' she whispered. Brent could feel Kathy at his side. Feel her like a live firecracker. ''I wanted to do what I could to take your mind off things.''

''Marla—''

''Are you still doing the benefit on Friday? I thought they'd cancel, but everyone thought it was such a good cause, and Johnny wouldn't have wanted anyone to cancel it because of him. Brent, I really need to talk to you. Maybe we could go together.'' Marla did have her talents. The purr of her voice was so sensual she might have been stripping as she whispered her words. It didn't matter. If she knew something, he wanted to know what, and he didn't mind playing a few games to find out what.

''All right, Marla.''

''I'm afraid that won't be possible.''

Kathy, stepping around him, spoke at last. She wore a wonderfully sweet smile as she addressed the very startled Marla.

"Pardon!" Marla muttered, glancing from Brent to Kathy in confusion. Then she stared hard at Kathy and gasped. "You're her! You're his ex-wife."

"Yes, I'm her, all right," Kathy said sweetly with just a touch of sarcasm. "And I'm afraid he can't accompany you because I'm accompanying him."

"No, you're not," Brent muttered.

"Yes, I am," Kathy said. They were both smiling at Marla over clenched teeth.

Kathy smoothly offered Marla a hand. "And you're Marla Harrington. I've heard so much about you. It's a pleasure to meet you."

"Thanks. I, uh, I didn't know that you and Brent were still on friendly terms."

"Oh, very friendly, at the moment," Kathy said sweetly.

"Really?" Marla said awkwardly. Then the situation was eased as Kevin Terrill, Brent's manager, made a sudden appearance, along with Pat Lacey, his press secretary. Both men were demanding to know where Brent had been and why he hadn't contacted them. Then they both recognized Kathy, and it seemed there was a lot of confusion.

Johnny's sister was led away, sobbing, and the caretakers made it pretty obvious they wanted everyone to leave so they could fill the grave.

Marla made it back to Brent for a brief moment. "Brent, darlin', I've really got to talk to you!" she whispered huskily.

Did she know something? Brent wondered. Anything?

"Sure," he said, squeezing her hands. "Sure, we'll get some time alone together. I'll see you on Friday."

She turned and left him. He started to turn away only to find Kathy standing there, staring at him. She looked so sophisticated. Elegant, beautiful—and very cold. Her smile was glacial. For such a tiny person, she could appear very superior.

"Brent, darlin', are you ready to leave? I believe that Robert is waiting for us. And the police aren't staying around much longer so the fans will be free to attack you if someone more—or less—lethal doesn't decide to first."

"I'm ready, Ms. O'Hara." He took her hand and led her toward Robert's car, his strides purposely long so she had to run on her high heels to keep up with him.

She was silent during the drive home while Robert quizzed Brent about the funeral. "I didn't find out anything," Brent said. "Well, I did find someone willing to talk, but Kathy rather nicely put an end to that."

"Oh, darlin', I don't think talking was what she had in mind."

"I have to find out."

"That's your prerogative," she told him innocently.

By then they had reached the house. She thanked Robert sweetly and in a matter of seconds, she was out of the car, through the gate and hurrying up the walk to the front door.

"She? Marla Harrington?" Robert asked.

Brent nodded, watching as Kathy disappeared inside. "Yeah, I'll try to get through to her on Friday. I've got to talk Kathy out of going."

"You want to borrow some handcuffs? That might be your only chance," Robert warned him.

"Thanks." Robert got out of the car with Brent, but refused his invitation to come in. Brent locked the gate and patted Sam, then wondered if he wasn't being a little ridiculous with the security.

No. He'd just left Johnny's funeral and he wanted to stay alive. Life had become exceptionally intriguing once again.

He went into the house. Kathy was in the bedroom; the door was closed. He could hear her, though. She was on the telephone, setting up a date for a photo shoot in two weeks. Then she was on the phone again, easily hedging questions about him, making sure she had the studio time and the photographer she wanted.

He'd almost forgotten she had her own business.

"Brent?" she said on the phone. He shouldn't be eavesdropping, even if she was talking about him. Especially if she was talking about him and suddenly sounding very casual.

"Yes, well, I've heard from him, of course. He was concerned about Shanna. I'm sure he's fine. I don't really know. We are divorced."

Ah, divorced... But on very friendly terms, that was what she had told Marla.

He smiled and tried the door. It wasn't locked. He pushed it open and went into the room. She was stretched out on the bed. Her feet bare, she was lying there in her tailored white blouse and form-hugging linen skirt. She had freed her hair and it fell in soft tendrils and waves around her shoulders.

She glanced at him and rather quickly ended her conversation.

He cast off his jacket and stretched beside her. "Busy?" he inquired politely.

"Well, Patty is great, but she really handles the house and my time more than anything else," she said casually. "I had a few things to catch up with."

"Oh." Leaning on an elbow, Brent asked politely, "Any repercussions from all this hitting you?"

"No, no, not really. Well, of course, people are curious about you. I guess our past association is fairly well known."

"Our past association?" he echoed genially.

"Yes."

"Just our past association?"

"What are you talking about?" she asked irritably.

"Well, gee, Ms. O'Hara, I just got the impression we were dating again."

"Dating?"

"Friday night. You're accompanying me, right?"

"If you're going to go—"

"But I could have had a date!" he protested.

Her eyes flashed dangerously. "If you're going to stay in this house and make demands, then you don't get to date, too. Not while—"

"Not while what?"

"Not while you're . . . you're sleeping with me."

"Oh?"

The telephone started to ring, breaking the tension rising between them. Kathy quickly picked up the receiver, her eyes a crystal fire of warning. "Hello?"

Brent could hear that the voice on the other end of the wire was male. Kathy listened uncomfortably for several seconds. She looked a little pale. She glanced at him uneasily, then tried to glance away. She slipped a hand over the receiver and smiled at him pleasantly. "Brent, this is personal. I don't suppose you'd—"

She broke off as he slowly shook his head, his refusal brooking no argument. She flashed him a glance of pure fury and tried to resume her conversation.

"I'm sorry, I should have called you. It's just that things moved so swiftly. I'm fine, I'm really fine.

Shanna is away. Well, yes, I'm back now. No, I'm sorry, anything this weekend is really not feasible. I—"

She gasped as Brent suddenly pulled the phone out of her hands.

"Axel? Hi, Brent McQueen here."

"McQueen, what are you doing there?"

"Oh, just stretched out, resting for the moment. Kathy can't see you this weekend. She forgot to mention that she and I are on, er—what did you call it, Kath?—very friendly terms at the moment."

Kathy lunged at him. He swept an arm around her quickly, sliding his hand over her mouth as she tried to grind out a few rugged expletives. "Ooh! What was that, sweetheart?" he murmured loudly.

"What the hell is going on? What are you talking about?" Axel demanded. "Put Kathy on the phone this instant. Where is she now?"

"She's right here, lying in bed with me. But she can't talk right now. Her, uh, mouth is occupied, you know what I mean?"

A burst of rage from Kathy was spilling through his fingers. "Can't talk any longer, Axel. Boy, is she a tiger, huh? Talk to you soon." He slammed down the receiver, rather uselessly, he thought. For Kathy kicked and rolled and sent the phone flying to the floor with a loud clang. His hand slipped from her mouth and she managed to get on top of him.

"How could you? How dare you? I don't believe—"

"Hey!" he interrupted loudly, catching her flying
fists and quickly flipping her beneath him. She was
absolutely seething, her eyes pools of liquid blue fire,
her hair a blond tempest flying all around her in an
erotic tangle. She lay beneath him, hotter than flame,
her breasts rising fascinatingly with each angry
breath. She started to swear at him again and he
smiled slowly.

"You had no right—"

"I had every right!" he retorted.

"You did not!"

"No, no!" he protested. "You called these shots,
sweetheart. As long as I was sleeping with you, I
couldn't date, right? Well, the same holds true for
you, too."

"But I didn't—"

"You split up a date I was making with Marla."

"I didn't try to tell her what I was doing with you!
I didn't say—"

"That my mouth was occupied?" he demanded,
interrupting her.

"You bas—"

"Hey, Kath, don't make a liar out of me, huh?"
He couldn't resist. He lowered his head and kissed
her while her mouth was open. Kissed her with heat
and fever and just a little bit of fury and the sudden

explosion of passion that had come to him when he had heard her talking to another man.

She tried to wrench away from him, tried to shove his chest away. He didn't let her. His body sprawled over hers. He caught her cheeks with his hands, and he kept her mouth open, filling it with his tongue. She twisted and protested, and he knew that he could never let her go because the fires rising inside him were coming to combustible heights.

And then suddenly, she was kissing him back. Her fingers were almost painful as they threaded his hair; her nails raked down his back.

He broke away from her, his lips traveling down her throat, his touch opening her tailored shirt and baring the rise of her breasts. He drew out her fullness, his thumbs running over her nipples. The aureoles were nearly aflame, swollen, hard, puckered, ripe to his touch, to his tongue.

"I hate you!" she whispered. And he froze. But she moved against him and her head tossed on the pillow and she whispered, "I want you, Brent! I . . . want you."

He shoved up her skirt and rubbed his body down the length of hers. He ran his touch over the texture of her garters and stockings, and over the soft bare flesh of her thigh. He lifted her hips and nipped and licked the flesh at the heart of her desire over the erotic lace barrier of her panties. Then he rose and stripped them away in a frenzy and barely managed to rip open his buckle and zipper before lifting her thighs around him and plunging into her and filling her with the rage of desire that obsessed him.

He heard his ragged cries, heard the tumult of her heart with her every breath, and he rose even higher with the sounds of her whispers. Then her cries and pleas came moist and sweet against his ear.

When they reached their climax, her words were incoherent. He held her while she shuddered. His fingers curled tightly in her hair and he kissed her forehead gently, his lips trembling. "Damn... Kathy..." he murmured with anguish. Then he groaned and staggered to his feet. He zipped his pants and left her.

Kathy lay there, still and startled, for long, miserable moments, wondering how such ecstasy could bring such loss and such pain. She bit the back of her hands, tears forming in her eyes. She had said she hated him.

She leaped up and started to smooth down her skirt. Then she paused and stripped off all her clothing and donned a terry robe instead. She walked out and found him at the piano. He wasn't touching the keys. He was leaning over it, his palms pressed against his eyes.

She sat next to him. Startled, he glanced at her, then stared at the keys again.

"Brent! I didn't mean it!" she said urgently.

He looked at her again. "What?"

"I—I didn't mean that I hated you."

He smiled slowly, ruefully. "I didn't think you did," he said very softly. Then he really looked at her and saw all the hurt in her eyes. He slipped his arm around her and pulled her against him. "It isn't you, Kathy. It's me."

"I don't understand—"

"I don't want to hurt you."

"You didn't hurt me, Brent. You've never hurt me, don't you understand? I—I wanted you." She paused, then whispered softly, "Desperately. Passionately. Deeply. You've never hurt me."

He stood suddenly, his back to her.

"Never?"

"Never." Again she paused. "Except when you left me," she admitted.

"I had to leave you," he said softly. Then he turned and came to her and gently massaged her temples.

"Why?" she whispered.

"I couldn't stay after what happened."

"But you didn't do it, Brent, you didn't."

His hands went still. "I wish I could believe that," he said quietly. He turned away from her and she knew he had ended the conversation, and that she hadn't reached him at all. She stood up to follow him, determined to get through.

"Brent—"

"I saw some steaks in the freezer earlier. Want to do them on the grill? They come out best half frozen."

"Sure. Fine. Brent—"

"Kathy," he said curtly, "we've barely been back together at all, and already we're fighting like cowboys and Indians."

"Well, hell, it's not that bad!" she protested. "You started it."

"I did not."

"You definitely did. You snatched the phone away from me and said really horrible and crude things to Axel. I don't think I'll ever be able to talk to him again."

Brent took the steaks out of the freezer. "Good."

"Good? You and I are just playing house, remember. What happens to my life when this is over? Assuming we have lives left, of course."

"Well, you don't date Axel again."

"He's a very nice man."

"Yes, yes, he's fine. But I told you, Kathy. You deserve someone wonderful."

"Do I? What about you and the lady of the draping body?"

"There's nothing between Marla and me. I told you that."

"And I told you that Marla doesn't know that."

"Yes, you dealt with Marla very well."

"At least I wasn't crude."

"Ah! The difference between us!" he exclaimed.

She threw up her hands in exasperation. Then she smiled, because at least he was smiling again. She walked into the kitchen and stood on her toes to kiss him lightly on the lips. "Steaks sound great. I'm going to take a shower and change. A bloody Mary would be great, too, if you wouldn't mind fixing me one. I'll be out in a few minutes. Okay?"

He nodded. "One bloody Mary."

She started toward the bedroom. At the door she paused and called to him. "Brent?"

"Yeah?" He stood by the counter and watched her. His hair was ruffled and a little long over the collar. His shirt was in slight disarray, but he still looked great with his tall, lean, broad-shouldered physique, strong, handsome features and piercing, whiskey-colored eyes.

"You know what?" she asked him huskily.

"What?"

"You are wonderful," she said quietly. "Really wonderful." She grinned. "Even if you do say so yourself."

Then she slipped into the bedroom and closed the door. It might be good to let him think about the precise meaning of her words.

The phone was giving off a dull buzz from where it lay on the floor. She picked it up and set it on the nightstand. Then she smiled again and hurried to the shower.

## Chapter 8

After she'd showered, Kathy pulled back the curtains on the bathroom door and looked out. Brent had the barbecue going. He'd changed to a pair of cutoffs and was stoking up the coals.

She started out of the room, then noticed the bathing suit in the little wicker trash basket. The basket was clean; the two pieces of the bikini were the only things in it. It was Shanna's bathing suit. Kathy couldn't let him throw it away. And she was really in the mood to torture him—just a little bit.

She rinsed the bikini, wrung it out and slipped into it. After grabbing a towel, she casually sauntered onto the patio.

He was no longer standing by the barbecue; he had moved closer to the pool to stretch out on one of the redwood deck chairs. From this position, he could see all of the forty-by-sixty pool, the screened dome enclosure and the patio plants within it, and the yard and the wall beyond. It was very private.

He was wearing sunglasses and sitting with a can of beer and the sports section from the newspaper. But as soon as Kathy stepped out, he swung around so swiftly that she cried out, startled. He might be sitting casually, she thought. But he was ready for anything.

"It's just me," she said. She couldn't see his eyes because of the sunglasses but she felt he was staring at her. "You were out here, so I was assuming you felt it was safe."

He still didn't say anything. She strolled over to the next deck chair and tossed down her towel. "Did you make my bloody Mary?" she asked him.

He gestured toward the round, glass-covered, wrought-iron patio table by the barbecue. She thanked him sweetly.

When she turned to take a seat, she found he was still watching her. He spoke at last. "I thought I had trashed that suit."

She arched a brow delicately over the rim of her glass and took a bite out of her stalk of celery before replying. "Trashed it? Oh, well, I did find it in the wicker basket. I thought it must have fallen there accidentally.''

"It wasn't an accident.''

"Oh? You don't like the suit?''

"Not on you.''

"Thanks a lot.''

"I didn't mean that,'' Brent said flatly. "What I mean is that it . . . it displays too much.''

"Brent, really, no more than any other bikini—''

"All right. It's the way it displays what it does, then. Kathy, the damned thing is provocative as hell. You want old geezers jumping off their boats with their tongues stuck to the decks?''

She leaned back, smiling. "Only the old ones?''

"Kathy, you know something? There are times when you're a real little witch.''

She sipped her drink, hiding a smile. "No, I'm really not. I'm just trying to plan ahead. For the future, you know.''

He slipped his glasses down his nose and stared at her. "What future?''

"Mine. Well, you've absolutely destroyed whatever I might have had with Axel.''

"You should thank me for that.''

She ignored his comment. "So I'm going to have to go out looking, you know, so I might as well be as prepared as possible, right?'' She was trying to goad him. Into what, she wasn't certain, but it didn't seem to be working.

He smiled. "I promise to cut that thing to ribbons before I leave."

"But when you leave is exactly when I'll need it. Just how long do you think you'll be staying, anyway?"

"That's hard to tell, isn't it?"

"You really had no right to do that to poor Axel. I'm being an extremely understanding ex-wife. I'm doing my very best while you destroy my life—"

"I'm trying to preserve your life, remember. And you haven't really given me the impression I'm destroying your life. Damned if I didn't think you were having, er, fun at various times along the way."

"Oh, yes, you can be mildly entertaining."

"Mildly entertaining?" he asked pleasantly.

She smiled, set down her drink, walked to the far end of the pool and dived in cleanly. The water was just the right temperature, cool against the heat of the day.

Seconds later, she heard a splash behind her. She quickened her strokes and moved to the side of the pool. Seconds later, Brent emerged from the depths before her. With a hand on either side of her he held on to the side. He asked again, "Mildly entertaining?"

She tried to slip below the surface and swim around his legs. In a second he had her by the foot and he was dragging her up. This time, his sleek bronze body pinned her against the side.

She didn't speak. He kissed her and their lips were damp and cool from the water, but when his mouth parted hers, all the warmth rushed in. He kissed her throat and she wound her arms around him as he nibbled her shoulders, biting her flesh lightly, running the hot liquid of his tongue over the spot to soothe away the erotic little hurt. She leaned her head back as he teased her throat again, as breath dampened and warmed her earlobe and collarbone. Then she felt his thumb and fingers running along the band of the bikini. "Let's see, what is you've wanted to hear? This thing is incredible on you, sexy as all hell, provocative, evocative, titillating. Old men, young men, in-between men would all be drooling at the sight. I love it on you. Here. In private. And I am going to cut the damn thing to ribbons before I leave."

"You can't do that. It belongs to Shanna."

"Shanna! You mean you let her wear that thing?"

"She'll be eighteen soon. I can't stop her from using her own judgment. Besides, she looks absolutely dynamite in it. David loves it on her."

Brent leaned back, groaning. "This is getting worse and worse."

"Don't you remember being that young?"

"I remember you being that young. And I remember a few of your outfits, too. And I remember—"

"What?" Kathy demanded as he broke off.

He started to laugh. "I remember a few of your father's comments about them, too. It's frightening, 'cause I know exactly what David feels."

"What do *you* feel?" Kathy whispered.

His fingers moved below the waistband, erotically, intimately, against her flesh. If he wasn't holding her, she would sink. She leaned her face on his shoulder while he replied huskily, "This."

He pulled her closer against him, and she felt the mound beneath the fabric of his jeans, flush against her own sexuality.

She closed her eyes. But they flew open again as she heard a loud explosion. Like a gunshot. Then she heard the ferocious, deep, snapping growl of Sam's bark.

Brent swore. Kathy's eyes widened. "It's probably just that car backfiring again," she said.

"Kathy, that was a damned gunshot, and the bullet ripped into the water somewhere!"

"Oh!"

By now, Sam was sounding like a wild thing. The Doberman had rushed around the dome enclosure to the back wall.

Brent let out a loud expletive, grabbed her hand and dragged her to the steps. "Stay the hell down!" he warned her. Dripping, he raced across the patio, dragging her behind him. He paused briefly at the table that held the steaks and swept up a kitchen towel.

She realized his pistol was beneath the towel. Her heart started to hammer even more ferociously as they entered the house through the sun-room that led to the living room. Brent shoved Kathy toward the kitchen. "Get down and stay there!" he warned her briefly.

"Wait! Where the hell are you going?" she demanded.

"Get down, Kathy! I am not playing duck shoot for anyone!"

She grabbed his arm, but he was gone. "Brent!" Terrified for him, she raced through the sun-room. Through the French doors, she could see that he had already reached the back wall, that Sam was barking like crazy as Brent scaled it. He disappeared over the wall, and there wasn't anything she could do.

Call the police.

But even before she had taken two steps toward the phone in the kitchen, Sam started barking again. Kathy froze, watching the Doberman tear around from the back of the house to the front. She held still, paralyzed, then she tore to the front door and stared through the peephole.

It was Robert. Worn, tired, in his rumpled business suit, he stood there, waiting, keeping as far away as he could from Sam.

She gasped with relief, leaning against the door for a second. Then she remembered that Brent was out there, and she threw open the door as quickly as possible. She set the alarm code to off and raced to the gate, swinging it open desperately.

"Get down, Sam! Robert! There was a shot. We were at the pool. Someone took a shot at us and then Brent went after him!"

"Where?" Robert said tensely.

"To Mrs. Fenniman's. The neighbor's yard. Around that way."

"Keep that damned dog with you, Kathy. Get back in. I'll go around."

He shut the gate, pulled his gun from his shoulder holster and went off. Kathy bit her lip, wishing she was with them instead of being left alone.

She gripped Sam by the collar. "Come on, Sam. You come in with me. You're the only male I really trust." She remembered how he hadn't let out a peep while Brent silently broke into the bathroom. "Never mind. You're a traitor, too, but you're all I've got for the moment."

She brought the dog into the house. The air conditioning made it cool. She was wet and shivering, but she couldn't bring herself to move. She felt numb. Brent was out there. He had gone tearing after a killer, so it seemed. He shouldn't have done that, he should have stayed in the house. He could get himself killed.

He had to do it. She knew Brent so well, and she knew he would never sit still while others took crack

"You're going to listen to me from now on!" he muttered fiercely, striding quickly by her. He keyed off the alarm again and went to the gate to meet Robert. Kathy followed him to the door. She watched as the two men talked for a moment, then Robert walked to his car. He must be using the radio.

Then the two men walked up to the house. Robert was still asking Brent to describe the man, but there was nothing much Brent could tell him. The man had been about medium height, medium build, thirty to forty years old, dark hair. He had disappeared into the bay in a motorboat.

"Well, we may get him," Robert said. "Even if we do, sounds like a hired job to me. I don't know what we'll get out of him. I do think I've got something for you, though."

"What?" Brent demanded. He opened the refrigerator and pulled out a pitcher of tea. He held the cold container against his face for a moment before walking across to the cabinet for glasses. "Anyone want to join me?"

Kathy shook her head, Robert accepted. He sipped the tea, then leaned over the counter. "We found a few guys at the state prison who were willing to talk about Harry Robertson."

"And?" Brent demanded.

"Seems like Harry was always saying he was going to be okay once he got out. That he had the real prize stashed away somewhere. He'd had a partner, the guy who had gotten him into the smuggling to begin with. He felt that the partner had ruined his life, then let him take the rap all by himself. But he was going to get even with the partner. He was never going to let the guy find the real treasure. The one guy, Harry's cellmate, seemed to think that there's a warehouse vault in Miami somewhere with Harry's treasure in it.''

"What does that have to do with Brent?" Kathy asked.

"Someone in the band knew the combination to the lock on the warehouse vault. And it has something to do with Brent. Harry said so.''

"What?" Brent demanded.

"You've got the number somehow, someway. You're the one who's got it.''

"So why try to kill Brent? Why kill Johnny?"

Robert shrugged. "Johnny had a reputation. Maybe Harry's partner thought Johnny knew something. And knowing Johnny, he might have kept his mouth shut but told this guy—the partner—to kiss off. Maybe the partner didn't give warnings. I don't know. But at least you know a little more about what's going on, Brent.''

Sure, they knew a little more, Kathy thought bitterly, but what good was it? They couldn't even go outside without someone taking shots at them. And

Brent was still insisting on going to the benefit on Star Island.

She heard sirens. "There are the patrol cars," Robert said. Kathy looked at him with alarm and he smiled. "It's all right, Kathy. They're going to look through the woods out back, down to the water, to see if they can find something. Then we'll need to fish the bullet out of the pool. Ballistics might help, you never know."

Kathy nodded. Brent had disappeared into the bedroom and reappeared with her terry robe. He tossed it at her with a scowl. "Put that on, will you, please?" he demanded fiercely, then started out the door, holding Sam by the collar. Robert shrugged at Kathy and followed Brent to meet his officers.

Kathy checked the barbecue grill. The coals had died, so she brought the steaks in and threw them into the refrigerator.

Darkness came. Eventually Brent and Robert returned with other officers, and Kathy sat and answered what seemed like ridiculous questions while Brent went with one of the men into the pool to look for the bullet.

At midnight she made coffee and sandwiches. They found the bullet, then checked the grounds again. The officers left.

Brent and Robert sat on bar stools, talking. Brent was clean again; the water in the pool had washed away the dirt and grime from his skin. Robert was insisting that Brent think, and Brent was growing irritable, telling Robert he didn't have any damned solutions. It was going to go on for a while, Kathy decided.

"I'm calling it a night, guys," she told them. They looked at her blankly and she started down the hall for the bedroom.

Robert called after her. "Kathy?"

"What?"

"You should be thinking, too. You were on that tour with everyone else. You might know what Brent knows."

"I don't know anything!" Brent flared.

"All right. So the killer may think Kathy knows whatever he may think you know. So anything, anything at all, you call me, Kathy."

"Sure, Robert. Good night."

In the bedroom she stripped off the robe and the bikini and crawled into an oversize tailored shirt and slipped beneath the covers. She wanted to wait for Brent, but as she lay there, her eyes closed. He would wake her, she thought. If he wanted, he would wake her.

But he wasn't coming in that night. Somehow she knew it.

She dozed. She awoke a few hours later and saw that it was almost three. He hadn't come in. She closed her eyes and slept again, and when she next awoke, sunlight was filtering through the curtains and bathing the room in a golden glow. She rose and washed her face, brushed her teeth and combed her hair. Then she walked to the living room.

He was on the couch. He hadn't changed. He was still in his cutoffs, his arms crossed over his bare chest. His eyes flew open as she stared at him.

He sat up, startled. "Morning, huh? Already?"

She nodded. "I'll start the coffee. Want anything to eat?"

He nodded and stood. "Yeah, toast and bacon and eggs, sunny-side up. You feel like doing it?"

She nodded. "Well, it seems that the rest of my activities have been curtailed. I might as well."

"Thanks." He stared down the hallway. The phone began to ring. "I'll get it," he called to her.

Kathy went into the kitchen and started the coffee.

Brent picked up the receiver in the bedroom and after his initial "Hello?" went rigid.

"McQueen. You've got something of mine and I want it. You understand?"

"Who is this?" Brent demanded heatedly.

"No, McQueen, no way. I know that there's a tap on this phone and I'm not staying on long enough for a trace. You just find what I want. Your wife will go first. Then your daughter. And don't ever kid yourself. I can get to her. You just can't hide from me. Find what I want."

"What the hell is it you want?"

"The number. I want the number. Soon. I'll give you until the benefit, then I want that number!"

"You sure as hell aren't going to get it if I'm dead. And someone was shooting at me."

"Warning shots. Next time, it won't be a warning. Next time, we'll take your wife. And if you don't give us what we want, you won't get her back. You understand?"

The phone line went dead. Brent jiggled the phone, then called Robert's office. Robert wasn't in, so Brent talked to one of the detectives, who apologized. They had gotten the husky, sexless whisper of the caller on tape, but they hadn't had time to run a trace. Brent thanked the man and hung up.

His hands were covered in a cold sweat. The caller couldn't get Kathy. No one could, not here. It was just that the thought of it . . .

And he had said he could get Shanna, too, that they couldn't hide.

He slammed his fist against his hand in raw, helpless fury. He had to find out what the hell was going on. None of them was safe if he didn't.

He picked up the phone and called the police station again. Robert had come in by then. He agreed to send a few plainclothesmen to stay with Kathy while the two of them set out together.

Brent rose and showered and dressed quickly. He went into the kitchen. Kathy had coffee poured for him and the scent of the sizzling bacon was delicious. He sat, wondering how to tell her casually what he was doing. He didn't want her to know about the call.

The phone started to ring again. He made a leap for it but the wall phone was right next to the refrigerator and Kathy picked it up. She looked at him, startled, when he nearly crawled over her.

"I'll get it," he said.

"I've already gotten it," she said to him. Her eyes remained on the receiver while she said, "Hello?"

She listened for a moment, her smile growing plastic. "Yes," she said at last. Then she thrust the phone at him.

"Who is it?"

"Marla Harrington. I was going to tell her that your mouth was occupied but I don't think she would have cared. She's insisting on talking to you. She's terribly sweet. She told me that she'd see me Friday, too, but I'd have to understand that there were things between you two and she needed some time alone."

Her plastic smile remaining in place, she thrust the receiver into his hands. He watched the rigid squaring of her shoulders as she walked away.

"Hello?" he said to Marla.

He didn't hear her answer at first. Kathy had turned around, and as he watched her, the voice on the phone seemed to fade. In the long tailored shirt that reached down to her upper thighs, her hair pulled back in a loose ponytail, her makeup all scrubbed away, and with her back nearly arched and her claws just about showing, she was a picture of dangerous appeal. Her eyes flashed at him, beautiful deep blue, and little tendrils of her hair curled around her classic features, framing them.

"Brent, are you listening to me?" Marla was saying.

"Uh, yes, yes, I heard you." What the hell had she said?

"I'll talk to you more at the benefit, but I know Johnny thought you knew something, too. I think Johnny knew exactly what was going on, but he didn't believe what the consequences would be until it was too late. Brent, I do think you have the key somewhere."

She wasn't telling him anything, Brent thought wearily. Just the same old stuff.

"Yeah, sure, thanks. I'll see you Friday," he said, then told her goodbye and hung up. Kathy had laid out the plates. He sat down and sipped his coffee, watching her.

"There really isn't anything between Marla and me, you know."

"Hey, what's it to me?" she said sweetly. She took a delicate bite of egg, then smiled at him. "But if you touch that bathing suit, I'll break your arms."

He smiled and set down his fork. "When I leave, it's coming with me."

"A present for Marla? Not on your life."

He groaned and bit into a piece of bacon. They heard Sam start to bark, and the bell out by the gate began to ring.

Brent leaped up. Kathy looked at him, her eyes widening suspiciously.

"I've got to go," he said.

"Where?"

"It's all right. Someone is coming to stay with you, and I'm going to my place and to my studio with Robert. I'm going to go through every damn thing I have and try to find out whatever this number is that's causing all of this."

"If you find a number, what good will it do you? There are numbers on everything. What good is a number?"

"Kathy, I've got to go. I'll be back later."

She thought he was going to kiss her, but he didn't. He paused, then walked to the door.

A few minutes later, there were two young men in jeans and T-shirts at the door with Brent. One was working very hard on getting to know Sam. The other offered her his hand and a grin.

Then Brent was there, behind the two. "Kathy, these are Detectives Clinton and Barker—"

"Jerry," the darker of the two said.

"Steve," the second told her, reaching out a hand. They were both young and friendly and smiling with open admiration.

Kathy realized she was barely dressed. Brent was less than subtle about it. "Kathy, will you please go put something on?"

She flashed him a furious gaze. "I wasn't expecting company, remember?" she asked sweetly.

She stared at him then turned. His gaze remained implanted in her mind—the condemning, hard gold in his eyes, the tightness in his features. She strode into her bedroom and pulled out shorts and a tank top. Then she sat on the bed, a tempest of emotions roiling within her.

Damn him! He didn't want her, but it seemed he didn't want anyone else to have her, either. She should call Axel and apologize.

But she didn't want to apologize. And even as she wondered just what the relationship was between Marla and Brent, she knew she really didn't care about Axel. Oh, she did, as a friend. He was a very nice man, a good man. He just wasn't...wonderful.

And Brent was.

She rose and dressed, and when she came out, she offered the plainclothesmen coffee and breakfast, but they had just eaten. They were both great guys, easy, relaxed. Still, they were making her a nervous wreck.

She tried to work. She did manage to plan a few layouts. She talked to Patty and found out her picture had been in the paper. She had been standing next to Brent at the funeral and people were speculating.

There was nothing to speculate about, Kathy assured her. She asked Patty to sit tight. The police wanted them under guard for a while, that was all.

She hung up and tried to work again. She wanted to talk to Shanna, but she knew she couldn't.

She was sitting there, still trying to work, when the phone rang. She answered it and was surprised to find that the caller was Marla Harrington again.

"Kathy, is he around anywhere?" Marla asked her.

"Uh, no, not now. Why? What is it?"

"I just wanted you to know..." The other woman hesitated.

"Know what?" Kathy demanded, exasperated.

Then Marla started to talk in a rush. "I care about him, you know, I really care about him. I'm not trying to cause trouble or anything like that. It's just that...you hurt him. You're bad for him. He was just starting to get a new life. You should...you should leave him alone!"

"Marla, I'm sorry, I don't know what to say to you. I didn't come to Brent. Brent came to me."

"You don't understand. I don't know what he's said to you, but it may not be the truth. He's trying to protect you, but...he's going to marry me. He asked me to marry him. We weren't exactly living together, but we were together most nights. Don't get involved. You'll hurt everyone."

"Marla—"

The phone went dead. Kathy hung up.

The woman was lying. Kathy was certain of it. Brent had said he wasn't sleeping with her. He had said he had *never* slept with her. Hadn't he? Or had he evaded the question? She couldn't remember.

She pressed her head between her hands. Someone was lying. It wasn't Brent. He didn't lie to her.

Or did he? He had never pretended he was staying. He was trying to protect her. If she loved him, she should believe in him.

She loved him. She had always loved him. That didn't mean he loved her, and it didn't mean he was sworn to tell the truth.

"Hey, Mrs. McQueen." It was Steve, tapping on the door to her bedroom. "Are you a poker player?"

She smiled at him. "Sure."

She played poker with Jerry and Steve. She made lunch, dug out her *Casablanca* tape and her colorized version of *King Kong* and they argued over the merits of both.

The day passed. She thought about calling Brent's house and his studio, but every time she picked up the receiver, she put it down again.

In the evening Jerry went out for pizza and they agreed on everything but anchovies and cold beer. At one o'clock she thanked them both and said she was going to bed. They both assured her it was one of the nicest assignments they had had.

She went to bed and lay awake for a very long time. Then she closed her eyes and dozed restlessly at last.

He wasn't coming back.

But he did. Sometime in the night, he returned. Though he didn't touch her as he had before. He didn't try to make love to her.

He lay on his back, looking at the ceiling. She opened her eyes and saw him there. She didn't know if she wanted him to touch her, or if she was afraid that he would. She wanted to ask him the truth about Marla, but couldn't quite bring herself to do so.

His eyes closed. She turned her back on him. A few minutes later she felt his arms around her, pulling her close.

He didn't make love to her. He simply held her in the curve of his body, and she could feel the heat and security of his naked body wrapped around her.

She lay awake for a very long time.

## Chapter 9

Kathy awoke in the morning to music.

She was alone in bed. Brent was at the piano playing the chords to "Forever My Love." She got up, showered and dressed, hoping that he would have quit playing the tune by the time she reached the living room.

He had. When she came down the hallway, he was still sitting at the piano, but he did so silently, his hands idle on the keys.

"Hi," he told her morosely.

"Hi."

"Coffee is already on."

She nodded and walked by him into the kitchen. She poured herself a cup and came out. She wanted to talk to him, really talk to him. She wanted to tell him about Marla's call and demand to know the truth.

And of course, she wanted him to tell her that Marla was behaving like a child, trying to destroy things for them.

Destroy what? Could anything be more broken and shattered than their relationship? These few days were just an interlude. No one had ever pretended they were anything else.

*No.* They were pretending that these days would pass, and then nothing more would follow. She had to talk to him.

But it didn't seem to be the time. She didn't have his attention. "So you didn't find anything at your place? Or at the studio?"

He shook his head. "Robert seems to think that I must have a paper or something stashed away. Something Harry gave me. And there's nothing." He hesitated. "I just keep coming back to the song." He shrugged. "Tomorrow's the benefit. Maybe something will come from that."

"Maybe," she agreed. She shrugged. "If you want, I'll play around with the song, too."

"I thought you hated it."

"Yes, well, it seems to be all our skins that we're dealing with here, doesn't it? And I never hated the song. I just hate to hear it now."

It seemed that she had his attention at last. He was watching her, his eyes gold and curious and his smile wry and crooked. "Why is that?"

She started to answer him, but they were startled by the sound of Sam's ferocious barking.

Kathy arched a brow at Brent. "Robert?"

He nodded. "One more day of searching through records and notes and all. Kathy, I've got to figure out what the hell it is that I supposedly know."

She nodded. He rose and came toward her. He pulled her into his arms.

For a moment, she stiffened. For a moment she could see Marla Harrington with him in that video, and she could hear the woman's voice coming to her urgently over the phone. Maybe she was just hurting Brent and herself. Maybe this was insane.

But he was touching her. And she seemed to melt in his arms. They were hard and secure around her and his lips were achingly tender when they touched hers. He kissed her slowly, lingeringly, then he stepped back and brushed the moisture from her lips with his thumb. "I'll be back."

"Will you?" she asked him softly.

He frowned. "Of course. Why?"

She shook her head. "No reason. I'll . . . I'll play with the song."

"Your two little friends are back, you know."

Her lips curled into a smile. "Little?" Detectives Jerry Clinton and Steve Barker were both over six feet tall.

Brent shrugged. "Well, they're just kids, you know."

"Mmm," she agreed. "Very attractive ones. And actually, I imagine that they're both at least in their mid to late twenties. Mature, responsible—"

"And duly impressed with your charms. Behave," he warned her. "I heard all about that poker game."

"Hey, I won."

"Yes, that's what I heard. They were having problems concentrating."

She smiled. "Bye. Have a nice day. And you behave, too."

"I don't have much choice. Poring through drawers with Robert doesn't give me many opportunities to practice my wicked ways."

"Ah, but is Robert the only one around?"

He frowned. "Kathy, what are you talking about?"

She shook her head. "Never mind. We'll talk later."

"Yes, we will," he said flatly. His eyes remained on hers. They could hear Sam going into a frenzy. Brent sighed and turned. "It'll probably be late," he said.

Something about the tone of his voice bothered her. There was a weariness to it, and a desperation. Maybe something more. She felt a cold hand squeeze her heart. Was it because of the things going on between them? Passion had risen so quickly, and now it seemed that the embers were cooling as fast.

"Brent, there's something you're not telling me," she said flatly.

He swung around, staring at her, and she knew she was right.

"My God, it's true!" she whispered, backing away from him.

"What's true?" he demanded, following her.

"The phone call—"

"How the hell do you know about the phone call?" he demanded brusquely.

"Because she called me!" Kathy flared. "That's why!"

"She!" He stopped dead in his tracks. "How do you know it's a she?"

"Oh, come on, Brent! Are you trying to tell me now she isn't a woman? Oh, my God! This is getting worse and worse. Just go. Go and—"

"Kathy!" He caught her shoulders, pinning her against the wall. "Kathy, what the hell are you talking about?"

"Marla."

"Marla is the one killing people and making all these threats?"

"What?" Kathy gasped.

He shook his head. "Wait, wait, we've got to start all over again. Who called you? What call are you talking about?"

"What call are *you* talking about?" she challenged him.

"Kathy, what—"

"Marla. She said you'd been having a really hot and heavy affair and that you were going to marry her."

He groaned and released her shoulders. Then he leaned against the wall, laughing.

"Brent!" Kathy snapped furiously.

"I'm not marrying Marla, all right? And any hot and heavy affair I've had with her is in her mind. She was a friend. I worked with her. She's usually a nice kid. Actually, I thought she was after Johnny. I've been places with her, yes. But she called you and said I was going to marry her?" he said incredulously.

Kathy nodded.

"And you believed her?"

She shrugged. "I was going to ask you about it."

"Well," he said softly, "that was good of you. If she calls back, hang up on her." He paused. "No, don't. She thinks she knows something. Talk to her. See what she says, all right? I've got to go."

He started to leave, then stopped, came back and kissed her. "Actually, I'm not supposed to owe you an explanation like that. I'm only supposed to behave while I'm actually sleeping with you," he said huskily.

"Well, it's just that you did so well in destroying my relationship with Axel," she said sweetly. "I'd hate to see you walk away from this untarnished."

He laughed. "But we've agreed. Axel isn't wonderful."

"Mmm. And I suppose we've agreed that you are?"

"Hey, you said so," he reminded her. He started to kiss her again. Sam was going crazy outside and the bell was ringing away but they ignored both. After a few moments, he finally pulled away regretfully.

"I've got to—"

"Wait!" she said swiftly, holding tight to his arms so he couldn't walk away. "What phone call were you talking about?"

A little shield seemed to fall over his golden orbs. "What?"

"Brent, what phone call—"

"We'll talk later. I've really got to go."

"No! Not until you tell me!"

He hesitated. "The killer called," he said with a sigh. "He wanted the numbers I supposedly have. He wants them by tomorrow night."

"Oh, my God! You can't mean—"

"I think it was a man. The call was very quick. The police weren't able to trace it."

"Brent—"

"I have to find the numbers, or whatever it is this maniac wants. Not to give to him, but to use to stop him. I have to, Kathy. Can you understand?"

"I understand that I'm scared," she whispered. "Maybe he gave Johnny a call just like the one he gave you. Brent, you shouldn't be out. You shouldn't go to that benefit."

"I have to go. You don't."

"If you're going, I am, too."

He swore softly.

Outside, it seemed that someone was sitting on the bell. Sam was barking himself into a spasm.

"We'll talk about it later," Brent said gruffly.

Seconds later, he was gone. Kathy leaned against the wall, then sank slowly against it.

"Mrs. McQueen?"

It wasn't her name. The cops should have known it wasn't her name. It didn't matter. She looked up and saw that Steve had come into the hall. Sam was with him, his tail wagging. Brent had introduced Sam very properly to Steve, and it seemed that the two were the best of friends.

"Hi, Steve."

"Are you all right?"

"I'm fine, thanks."

She smiled at him and let him help her to her feet. She said hi to Jerry, then excused herself and sat at the piano.

She began to play the song, humming it softly. She didn't have Brent's voice, and she didn't have his magical touch with musical instruments. But she knew the song. She knew it backward and forward, and she sang it softly.

I will love you forever, forever, my love.
Longer than the heavens ride the sky up above.
Deeper than the depths of the darkest seas,
Stronger than the life that breathes within me,
Forever, into time eternal,
Forever, into light, and into dark,
Forever, my love, forever, my love.
She comes to me like the breeze in the night
A touch, a whisper, in the twilight
And her perfume fills the air,
I breathe her hair,
A brush of velvet, stroke of silk,
I reach, and she is there
Whenever I see her face,
Whenever I feel her smile,
I know that time can never erase
The visions all the while
I touch her skin
The sun rushes in
I sit alone by the dock on the bay
And I know that there will never come a day
When I do not love you forever, my love
Forever, my love, I will love you.
Forever my love, forever my love.

The last notes of the song softly died away. Kathy remained at the piano, silent, still.

It was supposed to have been forever. That had been the promise between them. Why had they let things fall apart?

She was going to grow nostalgic and drip all over the piano keys, she thought. She couldn't do that. Not now. She was supposed to be trying to figure out the secret behind the song. Before tomorrow. But there were no numbers in the song.

She got up and wrote the words on paper and stared at them that way, but no numbers came to her. There weren't even any references to any particular place.

She stared at the words a while longer, then smiled at Jerry when he said he was going for Chinese food. She gave him an order for shrimp with lobster sauce, then suddenly leaped up and raced into her room, to the cavernous closet.

She dragged out all the boxes from the back. She'd saved everything about Brent, everything that had been written. She'd kept a scrapbook, which she'd given Shanna after the divorce, but she still had a copy of every article ever written.

She flipped through newspaper clipping after magazine article after newspaper clipping and finally found what she wanted. It had been the first

story about him in a major publication, written after "Forever My Love" had first been published.
He'd liked the interviewer and he had given the
woman a great deal of insight. Kathy had always
loved the article. She scanned it quickly.

There'd been so much analyzing done over the
song. Brent hadn't felt that the music was that startling or unusual, nor had he found the words to be
anything more than a simple statement from the
heart. The interviewer rather hit the nail on the head
when she said the lyrics and music just came together in a really beautiful ballad that touched the
heart. Brent would probably be known for it forever.

Kathy read on. He talked about writing on the
dock near his house, and there was a wonderful picture of a very young Brent with his lazy smile. He
said that it had just never come together for him until he'd met Kathryn, his wife. Maybe that was why
the song worked. It wasn't just a song. It was everything he felt in his heart and his mind and his soul.

She set the article down. There wasn't a thing
about numbers in the article.

She turned the page. There was a picture of her in
her wedding gown. It was a traditional snow-white
gown sewn in a Renaissance style. She wore a tiara of
pearls, and the veil fell behind her in a cloud. If she
had ever been beautiful in her life, it had been on
that day. The picture caught the blue of her eyes, the

soft blond of her hair. She might have been a fairy-tale princess with her knight at her side, except that her knight was incredibly handsome in a black tux, cummerbund and starched white shirt. And his eyes were heated, intoxicating gold as he smiled at her....

She closed the magazine. It was about to make her cry. And it hadn't told her anything at all.

A few seconds later, Jerry was at her door. "Shrimp with lobster sauce, at your service, Mrs. McQueen."

"Thanks!"

The day passed slowly. She couldn't remember hours ticking by so slowly. She thought about calling Brent to see how he was doing, but then she remembered that Brent had been called here. It was possible someone might manage to hear what they were saying, that she might lead someone to Brent.

She didn't call. She waited.

She tried to be lighthearted and relaxed and enjoy Steve and Jerry, but it was difficult. And then it was finally night, and she pretended she was exhausted. It seemed that she lay awake forever and ever, and when she finally fell asleep that night, it was as if she was dead. She didn't hear Brent when he came in.

In the morning, she awoke slowly, feeling more tired than she had when she went to bed. She could hear Brent in the living room talking to someone. She froze for a second, wondering if he was on the phone, if the killer had called. But then she heard

Robert's voice and she knew their friend was already at the house.

It was Friday. The day of the benefit.

She showered, dressed and went into the living room. Brent was sitting at the piano. Robert was leaning across it, talking intently, his voice low.

They both looked up, startled, when she appeared. "All right, what is it now?" she demanded.

"Nothing. Nothing, really," Brent told her.

"Nothing," Robert echoed solemnly.

She rubbed Robert's shoulder. "Didn't anyone ever teach you that it's a sin to tell a lie?"

They exchanged glances. Brent shrugged. "Our mystery man called back. He's going to give me a few days. Maybe someone will trigger something in my mind tonight."

"A few more days," Kathy murmured. "That's good of this guy."

"Well, we've got tonight."

"Yes, of course. Tonight."

"And you behave!" Brent warned her.

"Me?" she inquired innocently. "Why, Mr. McQueen, you just flirt your little heart out, anywhere you think it might do you some good. I'm just the ex-ball and chain, remember?"

He grinned at the tone of her voice, raising a fist in mock anger and warning. "There's so much I remember."

"And you behave. Who knows, I just might be able to flirt in the right direction, too."

It wouldn't hurt to keep him on his toes. Especially when she wanted to talk so badly. To sit down and say all the things she never managed to say all those years ago. He was still hers, but if they made their way through the clouds, he might just keep walking.

"Breakfast anyone? Or is it lunch? Thank God for the benefit. I'm starting to go mad in this house."

They agreed on lunch. It was almost a pleasant meal, almost an easy one. They decided to make pasta primavera. Brent and Kathy chopped and cooked and tripped over one another and Robert laughed and they talked over old times.

Robert stayed and stayed, and though Kathy knew that he, being a dear old friend, was guarding them, she really wished he would leave.

He wasn't leaving. He was coming to the benefit with them. He had his tux in the car. He'd be with Brent all night.

She was relieved, she supposed. She wanted Brent to be safe. But she was suddenly afraid. Something could happen, and she might never have the chance she wanted.

Her announcement that she was taking a bath failed to bring Brent into the bedroom. Men never appeared when you wanted them to, she thought mournfully, surrounded by bubbles. They only walked in by surprise, stealing away years of a woman's life, and nearly throttling her when she dared to scream at the intrusion.

She soaked until she was thoroughly pruned, gave up, dressed in sheer white rhinestone-studded stockings, white bikini panties and garter belt, and waist-hook white bra to accommodate her backless white cocktail gown. Like the stockings, the soft, swirling skirt of the dress was studded with rhinestones. She applied her makeup, decided on gold stud earrings and her small gold cross as her only jewelry. She was slipping the dress over her head when Brent at last appeared in the room.

He paused in the doorway, watching her. "Wow," he said softly.

She smiled. "Want to help me?"

"Put it on or take it off?"

"Put it on. You talked out there way too long to contemplate taking it off. I need the hook done in the back."

"All right. But only if I get to take it off later."

She turned her back to him, sweeping her hair up to show him the hook at the nape. He walked behind her and obligingly did the hook, but his fingers lingered upon her shoulders and his lips touched her bare back.

"You bought this ensemble for Axel?" He seemed to growl.

She was glad he couldn't see her slow smile. "He has wonderful taste in clothing."

He muttered something she didn't quite understand. There was a knock on the door, and Robert asked if they were about ready. Brent swore and replied none too politely that he'd be ready in a damned minute. "Run out and grab my tux, will you, Kath? I'll be right out of the shower."

"Yes, sir!" she said, saluting. She ran out, smiled sweetly to Robert, who was uneasily pacing the living room, lifted the tux off the couch and came back into the bedroom. She laid the tux out on the bed. Brent appeared a second later, the steam of the shower rising from his flesh. Kathy watched him dress, admiring him, suddenly wishing that they could forget the benefit. She loved the sleekness and the muscles of his long body. She loved the relaxed way he moved. And she loved the way he seemed so easy with her, as if the years had never been.

"Is this straight?" he asked her. He was in a traditional tux with a black vest, bow tie and elegant, old-fashioned shirt with ruffs at the cuff and pleats down the breast. He was fooling with his tie.

She nodded, feeling a lump in her throat. Poised on her high heels by the door, she could suddenly find nothing to say.

He walked toward her, smiling. He paused when they should have been hurrying, and he touched her cheek, then picked up her hand and kissed it. "God,

Kathy, you are beautiful. I've tried so many times not to remember just how beautiful."

"You're pretty beautiful, too," she said softly.

He groaned. "Oh, no. I knew the ruffs were too much."

She grinned. "No. Just beautiful. Not because of the ruffs." Her grin faded, and for a moment, there was no danger. Robert wasn't waiting for them, and there was no place they really had to be. The world had receded except for him. She whispered softly, "Brent, I love you. I love you so much."

An anguished looked appeared in his eyes. His features constricted and a shudder seemed to rip through him. Then he leaned his hands against the door on either side of her head and kissed her lips gently. The words that he whispered seemed to be torn from him. "I love you, too, Kathy. I've always loved you, I will always love you, no matter...no matter where we are, no matter how far apart, no matter how many years go by."

Her mouth went dry and she felt tears welling in her eyes. He loved her. He wanted her.

But he wasn't going to stay with her.

"Hey!" A fist thudded against the door. "What's taking the two of you so long? Hell, maybe I shouldn't be asking," Robert muttered. "Listen, you're going to have a nice long night after this event. You're divorced. You're not supposed to even

like each other any more, so will you please come
on!''

Bless Robert. She managed to smile into Brent's
eyes, and then she laughed, and he managed to
laugh, too, though the sound was just a bit pained.
He took her hand and swung open the door. Robert
almost fell in on top of them. "Finally," he said. "If
we're going to do this thing, let's do it!"

Kathy straightened Brent's tie. "You look great.
Truly undercover."

"Oh, honey, there's going to be so much security
there tonight nothing could possibly happen. I
promise."

"Let's do it then," Robert said.

Thirty minutes later they were in the full swing of
the party.

It was a massive event, held in a beautiful contemporary home with twenty-foot windows that
looked straight out over a huge patio and pool and
the bay. People in beautiful and garish and outlan-
dish costumes were posed all around—on stairways,
in hallways and on the patio. Kathy greeted old
friends, shrugged off her appearance with Brent,
tried to avoid those who were determined to pin her,
and at the same time keep an eye on Brent.

They hadn't been there for five minutes when
Marla found Brent. Kathy greeted her very sweetly
and didn't let out a murmur when Marla led Brent
away. After all, she just might say the right thing.

But still, Kathy didn't want him where she couldn't see him. Not because of Marla, but because she was worried. Even if Robert was following him like a leech.

A tuxedoed waiter swept by with champagne glasses. Just as Kathy reached for one, hands slipped around her waist and she felt a friendly kiss on her cheek. She managed not to drop the champagne, to thank the waiter and spin around all at once.

"Keith!" she said. She put her arms around him, still balancing the champagne, and hugged him tight. She had always liked him.

"Kathy, it's so good to see you. You know, Brent has never been the same. We've missed you. We've all missed you. But you're here tonight. Does this mean—"

"You know what this means," Kathy interrupted him. "Keith, I'm so sorry about your wife. And about Johnny."

"Johnny," Keith muttered. "Well, Johnny lived hard, and he died hard."

He sounded bitter, Kathy thought. He was a handsome man, with intelligent, dark brown eyes, dark hair, and the look of one of yesteryear's composers. Beethoven, perhaps. But tonight he looked haggard, drained.

"Kathy, want to talk, really talk?" he asked her suddenly.

"Sure."

He drew her outside. Workers were setting up for the bands and singers by the pool. Keith didn't want to be there. He drew her away from the house, into the trees. She followed him trustingly. He stopped at last, and he seemed to have difficulty breathing. "Kathy, do you know what's going on?"

She nodded. "Someone killed Johnny Blondell. Someone who grew angry. The same person who had Harry Robertson killed in jail. The same person—"

"Who probably killed my wife. Kathy, I was ill, I missed her so badly. But you know, this is terrible, I don't want to die myself. He's after a number. There's something stashed somewhere. Something of incredible value. And it's here and it's close, and we should all know it. Kathy, it's in the song."

She shivered suddenly, feeling the coolness of the night breeze rake up her spine. "How do you know?" she said.

"Johnny called me up and said he had some of it figured out but he'd be damned if he was going to be double-crossed. He wanted to talk to Brent. He was all excited. I think Johnny might have been halfway in it with Harry."

"But Johnny is dead."

"Harry probably didn't trust Johnny. Oh, I don't think Johnny was in on the smuggling. But Harry told him something. Brent was the only one that Harry really trusted. That's why I think he stashed this thing somewhere purposely, using numbers that would mean something to Brent.''

Kathy shook her head. "I've been through the song, Keith. I've been through it and through it and—"

"Brent has to come up with something! Or else we're all going to die, Kathy. We're all going to die."

"Kathy!"

Brent shouted her name, thrashing furiously through the trees. He snatched her by the shoulders, bringing her against his chest and staring furiously at Keith over her head. "What the hell are you doing, Keith?"

"Talking. I was just talking."

"So you dragged her out here."

Just then there was movement in the trees. Two guns were suddenly beneath their noses, held by hands attached to the arms of Steve and Jerry.

"We were with her all the time, Mr. McQueen. Honestly," Steve said.

"Hey, what the hell—" Keith began.

"We were watching you, too, Mr. Montgomery," Jerry promised him solemnly.

"Yeah, hell, Miami's finest," Keith muttered. He looked at Brent. "You used to be my friend. Why don't you really try to keep us all alive, huh?" Then he swept past them.

"Sorry," Steve said. "I guess we should have stayed in the bushes."

Brent shook his head, looking after Keith. "No, no, it's all right." He slipped an arm around Kathy's shoulder. "Let's get back in, shall we?"

They walked along a trail to the patio. Robert was waiting for them, watching them emerge from the trees.

"Everything all right?" he asked Brent.

"Yeah, fine," Brent told him briefly.

"Good. I'll stay with Kathy. You're on stage in a few minutes."

Brent nodded and disappeared. Kathy stood by Robert as a group of English brothers who had made it very big and bought property in south Florida came on. Their harmonies were legendary, and they put on a wonderful show. Kathy applauded enthusiastically. Then someone tapped her on the shoulder and she turned to receive a sloppy kiss and hug from each of the Hicks brothers.

Larry, blond and blue-eyed, looked her over openly, then grinned. "Okay, Kathy. Looking good. So you're together again. We're real glad."

Thomas nodded. He was the more serious of the two. "It's good to see you, Kathy. Really good. I hope we see more of you. Although I don't know. We haven't had a chance to talk about doing anything else about the Highlanders."

"Aren't you playing tonight?" she asked him.

He nodded again. "Yeah, sure. We just saw you and we had to stop." He looked around her shoulder to Robert and nodded cordially, but he was wearing a small frown. "It's the fuzz, huh?" he muttered to Kathy.

She smiled and nodded. "Yeah, I guess, you could say that. Robert, this is Thomas Hicks, and his brother, Larry Hicks, and—"

"Oh, hey, man, it's you!" Thomas laughed, greeting Robert. "I didn't recognize you in the duds, man. Lieutenant McGregor! Nice to see you. And thanks for being so conscientious. Those guys of yours have been with us like a second skin."

Kathy was staring at them all curiously. "We met," Robert explained to her. "I had to question everyone after the explosion that...that killed Johnny," he said.

"Oh, of course," Kathy murmured.

"We'll get together," Larry said. "We'll all get together. Maybe we can solve it that way, huh?"

He waved to Kathy, then he and his brother were weaving their way to the stage. A few minutes later, after a pop female vocalist had done her number, Brent, Keith, Larry and Thomas were announced— as the Highlanders. Brent was at the mike saying in his husky voice that they were dedicating the night to Johnny Blondell. And then they were doing Highlander numbers, and the crowd was going crazy.

At the end, Brent announced that he was going to do an old favorite. And he sang "Forever My Love."

fingers around the panties and pulled them off, leaving her clad only in the stockings and garters. She moaned softly, and he kissed her lips and breasts, and once again fell against the heart of her desire, only now there was no barrier between them. She cried out sharply, releasing everything to him, her head thrashing on the pillow.

He shed his trousers and briefs, shaking with the desire to plunge within her. Still he controlled himself, for she was so alluring with her hair spread in wild disarray, her flesh sheened from his lovemaking, her lips parted, her eyes shaded by the fall of her lashes, and the garters and stockings framing the wet, welcoming beauty of her sex.

He held back no longer. A strangled cry tore from his lips as he plunged deep within her to find a welcoming warmth close around him. Her eyes widened with the force of his entry, then her thighs locked around his hips. It seemed that the spark of desire, dying within her just moments ago, rose to life again on a rampant breeze. She squeezed him tightly, and he stroked and thrust with an increasing rhythm that seemed to bring the promise of climax closer and closer.

She met his thrusts with the arch of her hips. He ground against her. She cried out softly and he kissed her lips and breasts. When he knew he could hold back no longer, he caught her lips once again and filled her mouth with the desire and frenzy of his tongue as he filled her with the last shuddering force of his body and the stream of his seed. He felt her writhing beneath him, and he held her tightly in his arms until the spasms were over.

He wondered how anything could be so good and stay so good, and how she could electrify him time and time again. He knew it wasn't the wanting, it was the love, and that desire grew from that love.

But if it was so good, why had it all turned on them so painfully?

He held her closely. The seconds ticked by. She didn't speak, and neither did he. And when she would have spoken, he pressed his fingers against her lips and silenced her with his kiss. He made love to her again.

Later, much later, he felt the dampness on her cheeks, and he knew that she had been silently crying, but he couldn't say anything to her.

They had to get through this. And then he had to leave. There would be no way for him to change the past, no way for them to go back. No way to pretend he hadn't hurt her. And for himself, no way to pretend he wouldn't do so again.

All he could do was hold her and pray that the night would never end.

He was up, wide awake, leaning over her. She opened her eyes slowly—they didn't want to open. They hadn't slept at all. She hadn't minded, she hadn't wanted to sleep, she had wanted to touch him, to hold him, forever.

But the night had ended, and day had come.

His lips landed wetly and enthusiastically on hers, and then they were gone and his golden eyes were staring into hers. "You gave me the secret! Kathy, I think I've got it. I've got to get to my place and get the guitar. I've called Robert. He should be here any minute."

She groaned. "With Jerry and Steve, right?"

"Right. What's the matter with Jerry and Steve?"

"Nothing. They're real nice guys. Cute as buttons. You should worry about leaving me here alone with them."

"You're not coming with me. It could be dangerous for you to be out."

She groaned again. "Brent, if you're going out—"

"If I'm going out, I feel safer with you here."

The sheet fell from one of her breasts. His eyes slipped to the rise of her flesh, and he leaned over her to take her warmly into his mouth. Regretfully, he rose and smiled at her. "I'll be back."

"Promises, promises."

He was starting for the door. "Wait!" she cried. "You didn't tell me! What did you figure out?"

"I'm not sure yet."

"You think it's Keith, don't you? You were awfully rude to him last night."

"I don't think anything," he said coldly.

He turned and left. Kathy watched him and sighed. A few minutes later she heard the commotion at the door that meant Robert and his troops had arrived. She was exhausted but she knew she'd never be able to sleep. She felt exceptionally restless.

Because he knew something. He knew, but he wasn't sure, and so he wasn't going to tell her. But maybe someone else would think he knew.

The killer, perhaps . . .

She shot out of bed and hurried into the shower. Thirty minutes later she emerged from her bedroom to discover that Jerry and Steve had brought doughnuts and that they had gotten very good with her coffee maker and were smiling and eager to greet her.

They were both very nice. Dedicated, all American. That morning she spent drawing them both out and trying not to think about Brent. Jerry was one of five children. He'd spent three years in the navy, had lived in Miami all his life and wanted to change the city's image of being a hotbed for the drug and smuggling trades.

Steve was from a very small town in Alabama. He had a wife and a two-month old baby, and he simply loved the Miami area, the beautiful old homes and the foliage in Coconut Grove, the water that was always warm and always available. He even loved the action of the garish nightlife.

It was such a nice, easy conversation. Kathy didn't notice when it turned to her. There was nothing tricky or subtle about the change of subject. Jerry noticed a picture of Shanna and commented on what a truly stunning girl she was. And Kathy found herself laughing and agreeing and saying that yes, Shanna was their pride, both hers and Brent's. Then she was explaining how she had gotten into advertising, how she had worked while Brent struggled with music, how he had insisted they had everything, but that she should go back to school and take something that interested her. Sometimes her schedule had conflicted with his touring, but they had always worked something out.

Jerry was quiet, watching her. Then he blurted out, "It sounds so damned good. You were both courteous to one another. How the hell did you ever wind up divorced? No money problems, no religious differences. What happened?"

"Jerry," Steve groaned, sinking into his chair. "You gotta excuse my partner," he said.

"Oh!" Jerry said. "I forgot about your son—" He broke off, turning a mottled shade of red.

Kathy smiled gently, reached out and touched his hand. "It's all right. It wasn't Ryan, anyway."

"Then—" Jerry began.

"Stop!" Steve protested.

"It's just that—"

"Jerry!"

"It's all right!" Kathy laughed. "Jerry, I just can't really explain. It's too personal."

"You should still be married," Jerry said stubbornly.

"Well, you'll have to tell Brent that—" Kathy began but she broke off and they all stared at one another when Sam began to bark.

Then Jerry and Steve were up, both quiet and highly professional, guns drawn as they moved to see who was outside.

Jerry shoved his gun into his holster. "It's the lieutenant," he said.

"Oh. I'd better get Sam," Kathy said. She opened the door and called for the dog while Steve went to open the gate.

"Kathy, can you come with me?" Robert asked, watching Sam with distaste. "Brent needs to discuss something with you. I think he thinks he'll hit the last key to this thing if he has you with him."

"Of course!" Kathy agreed. "Let me grab my purse, and I'll be right with you."

She went into her room and dumped her wallet and brush and cosmetics from her evening bag into a big leather shoulder bag. She hurried to meet Robert, anxious to help Brent.

Why did she want to help Brent? she wondered. Once this was solved, he was going to walk out of her life. She was trying so hard with him, yet she wasn't getting anywhere. She had known that last night. She was going to start crying if she didn't hurry.

In the living room Robert was telling Jerry and Steve to hang around the house. He didn't know when he would bring Kathy back. With the phone ringing, he hurried her down the path and into his car.

"Think I ought to go back and get that?" Kathy asked. "It might be Brent." A cold finger of fear squeezed her heart. "You left him alone, Robert. Are you sure he's all right?"

"No, we don't need to get the phone, and yes, I'm sure he's all right," Robert assured her. "I left him all locked in where no one can get to him. Honestly."

He smiled at her. She smiled back.

Jerry picked up the phone. It was Keith Montgomery, and he seemed very agitated to discover that Kathy wasn't there. "What's the problem?" Jerry asked him.

"Well, I talked to Brent. He called from his house and he seemed upset. He wanted me to come over and stay with her, to make sure that she didn't leave the house for any reason. He had a hunch."

"He changed his mind," Jerry said. "He just sent the lieutenant to pick her up."

"That's not like Brent."

"The lieutenant's on the job, Mr. Montgomery. Just hold tight, and we'll get one of them in touch with you as soon as possible."

Jerry hung up. He looked at his partner and explained the call.

"Sounds like there's something wrong, doesn't it?" Steve said.

"Maybe we should get over to McQueen's place."

They looked at one another uneasily. Steve exhaled slowly. "Boy, our rumps could really be on the line here, you know."

"Yeah, I know."

Jerry shrugged. "What the hell. We can both go back to Alabama, right?"

"Yeah, sure, Alabama."

They left the house. At the last minute, Steve whistled to Sam.

Sam loved cars. He didn't hesitate a moment.

It wasn't long before Kathy realized they weren't heading toward Brent's house.

She'd never been in it. He'd bought it after the divorce, but she'd dropped Shanna off at the gate often enough, and she knew that though they were headed to the water, they weren't going to his house.

She frowned at Robert. "What's up?"

He shrugged. "We were down at the warehouses."

"By his old house, the small place," she breathed. "Where he wrote the song. So I was right."

"Yeah, yeah, you were right. And it had to do with that article you dug out, too. We're pretty damned sure. He was twenty-two when he finished the song, so he wanted to try the twenty-second storage unit. All he needed was the numbers to the vault."

"You're a cop, Robert!" Kathy laughed. "Can't you just blow it open?"

He shook his head. "I can't just go blowing up property of other citizens, can I? What if Brent is wrong about the numbers?"

"I guess you're right. But maybe you should get a unit down here or something—"

"Let's just see if Brent knows what he's doing first, huh?"

"Are you sure he's safe?"

"Oh, yeah. I'm sure."

They turned into the road that led to the warehouses. It was already twilight. The area was old and shabby-looking. Kathy didn't see a soul anywhere.

Robert pulled his car around back, close to the water. She looked at the docks. There were a few fishing boats pulled up to the pier and a few old motorboats. Darkness was falling quickly.

It seemed that no one had been to the warehouses in years. The paint was peeling. The scrawny grass and trees that wrestled a hold through the rocky earth were overgrown and mixed with weed.

"Come on," Robert said.

Kathy shuddered. "Boy, I wouldn't want to be here alone on a dark night," she told him. She cast him a smile. "Thank God I'm here with a cop."

He grunted. "Come on. Around this way."

He took her arm and led her to a small door in the rear of the brick enclosure. There was a padlock on it, but he pulled out a key and opened it. Kathy frowned, wondering what good the padlock would have done to protect Brent.

But before she could comprehend anything, Robert pushed the door open. For a moment, all Kathy could see was darkness.

Then she realized that Brent was in the room, gagged and on the floor in handcuffs. His ankles were cuffed, too, and chained to the wall. Kathy let out a scream and started to run for him but Robert caught her arm and wrenched her back.

"I told you he was safe," Robert said. "And he can stay that way." She heard a click and realized that he had pulled back the safety on his gun and had it aimed at her temple. "It didn't have to go down this way. Brent has the numbers, you see, Kathy. I could have taken the diamonds and—"

"Diamonds!"

"Yeah, it's diamonds. I came up with a connection in South America. And Harry Robertson and I had a deal. It's a long story. It started with a bribe at least ten years ago. Of course, I never let scum like Harry or Johnny Blondell know who I was. I didn't dare. And you would have never known. Except that once we got here, Brent seemed to figure something out. He started playing innocent. Then I caught him at the radio so I shot him.''

"Shot him!" Kathy gasped. He wrenched her closer, playing the cold muzzle of the gun over her cheek. "I grazed him. Had to knock him out. I couldn't risk a fight. He picked up too much about self-defense in the service. I just nicked his temple. He'll have a little bald spot for a while. But he'll be all right. If you can talk some sense into him."

Her eyes had grown accustomed to the darkness. She felt ill and terrified, aware that the loaded gun was against her head and that Brent was helpless on the floor. She didn't know if he was still breathing.

She couldn't comprehend that Robert... They'd gone to school together.

Then she realized that Brent was definitely alive. His eyes were open.

"He's awake," she said flatly. She had to stay calm. She couldn't panic. She had to reason with this man...when all she wanted to do was scream and scream and scream.

"Let him up. Uncuff him. I'll get him to give you what you want."

Robert kept the gun steady on her. He handed her a key. "You uncuff him. And remember, killing gets easier after the first. Not that I'd kill either one of you right away. A shattered kneecap can make lots of people talk really quickly."

Her fingers were shaking so badly she could barely undo the cuffs. Brent's eyes remained open, golden and warning on hers. She released his hands first, and he ripped off the gag and unlocked the steel cuffs on his feet. He staggered up and had to accept Kathy's help.

Blood trickled down his forehead from the gunshot wound. He faced Robert then, shoving Kathy behind him.

"I'll kill her. You know I'll kill her," Robert warned him.

"Yeah. And what guarantee do I have that you'll let us go once you have the diamonds?"

"None. But you know I'll blow you away if you don't."

"We're at a stalemate then, aren't we?" Brent said.

"No. Because I'm going to shoot Kathy somewhere within the next five minutes if we don't get the diamonds."

"All right. Let's go try warehouse number twenty-two," Brent said. "I don't have damned guarantees to give you, just an idea."

He started to stride by Robert, holding Kathy's hand tightly in his own, trying to keep her at his rear. Then he pushed her in front of them when Robert fell behind them.

It was almost completely dark. Shadows surrounded them. Kathy looked around Brent, still unable to comprehend that Robert could be at the root of all of this.

"Why?" she asked him incredulously.

"Why?" He smiled. "Have you ever taken a real good ride around here? Have you ever wondered how so many people can have so much money? Hell, the drug traders get off with good lawyers. The lawyers get rich on the drug money. Everybody's getting rich. I went so long without it, and then I just wanted a piece of it. There was a guy who needed to escape in the night. He gave me the location of some of his stash, and I took a chance. I let him go. And it was there, a whole cache of diamonds. And it was mine. Just for letting that thug go before the courts could do it instead. I learned a lot from that. But Harry Robertson turned out to be a pathetic little rat. And then he held out on me. I had to have him killed.

"But I want the diamonds. The game is up. They'll buy me a place and security for the rest of my life. I always liked you, Kathy. Always. I'm sorry. I wanted to keep you out of it. I didn't have any choice. Brent, open that damned door, now."

"You killed Keith's wife!" Kathy gasped, horrified.

"I thought Keith was the man at first. I needed to scare him. To get him off guard."

"So you killed her."

"And I'll kill Kathy," he reminded Brent.

Brent eyed him, then looked at the electronic combination lock. He played with some numbers. Nothing happened. Seconds ticked by.

Robert wrenched Kathy to his side and shoved the gun against her face. Tears stung her eyes. She could almost taste the metal.

"Now, Brent, now."

"Then what?" Brent demanded. "You've got the gun down her throat right now. What am I giving you the diamonds for?"

"All right, listen. You get me the diamonds. We leave Kathy here, and you come with me. She won't say a word to anyone because I won't let you go until we're far out at sea."

"Let her go now," Brent said.

Robert hesitated.

"Let her go," Brent repeated.

Robert shoved Kathy away. "Get down the walkway," Brent commanded her. "You stay away, you hear me?"

She nodded jerkily.

Brent pushed more numbers. The vault slid open.

Robert waved his gun in the air. "Get the diamonds."

Brent disappeared into the vault. Robert turned the gun on him. "Get over here, Kathy. Or I'll shoot him right now. He's too dangerous to take with me. It has to be you."

She stood still. He aimed his gun toward the vault. She cried out and raced toward him. A second later he had her in a hammerlock. "Give me the diamonds, Brent. And for every one that spills, she loses a finger. Push them along the ground."

Brent reappeared, staring at Kathy and Robert. He bent down and slid the velvet sack of diamonds on the floor to Robert. Holding the gun to Kathy's face, Robert stooped with her to pick up the satchel. Then he started to back away. Brent followed. Robert aimed the gun at Brent's face. Brent followed anyway.

They moved across the stone and the earth to the docks. And still Brent followed, keeping his distance. Then Robert stopped in front of a motorboat.

"Give me back my wife. You've got the diamonds, and you're free."

"Can't trust you, Brent, sorry," Robert said. There was about a three-foot drop between the dock and the boat. Robert shoved Kathy off the dock, and she cried out, landing hard on the boat's deck. He leaped quickly behind her, untying the rope that looped the boat to the dock. He stepped forward, his gun aimed at Brent, while he pulled the cord on the engine.

The small motor seemed to cough and wheeze and leap to life. "Stay there. She'll come back to you," Robert said.

"Like hell!" Brent swore. "You'll shoot her out at sea and dump her body. You won't have any other choice."

Suddenly, they heard the sound of barking. It was enough to distract Robert, if only for a second. In that split second, Brent leaped from the dock to the boat, landing on top of Robert. The gun went flying. And the boat moved from the dock.

Kathy staggered up from beneath the fallen men. The motorboat was spinning in circles as the two men viciously battled at her feet. She tried to slam her fists against Robert's back, but the boat careened, and both men went overboard.

In the murky darkness, she couldn't see either of them. They could be anywhere, beneath the motor...

With a scream she lunged forward and cut the motor. The barking was suddenly very fierce and she noticed that Sam was on the dock, going crazy. Jerry and Steve were behind him, searching the water with a flashlight.

The boat pitched precariously, catching her off balance. She tumbled into the darkness of the water and sank into the dark green depths.

There were fingers in her hair. Her lungs burning, she twisted and tried to see. Robert had her. And he was dragging her down.

But he was wrenched away and she kicked furiously, desperate for air. She surfaced. "Brent!" she screamed. He didn't come up. Someone touched her and she tried to fight. "It's me—Steve. Let me help you."

"No, no. Brent—"

"You can't help him. Don't you see? The lieutenant keeps using you against him!"

She let Steve pull her away. Jerry dragged her onto the dock and Steve went into the water. She breathed heavily, trying not to panic.

"It's all right, it's all right," Jerry was saying.

No, it wasn't. Brent wasn't coming up.

But then there was a burst from the water. Straining to see, she made out Brent coming to her with strong strokes. Sobbing, she sank to her knees and reached for him. Jerry reached for him, too, then Brent was up and out of the water, lying flat on his back on the dock. For long moments he gasped for breath with his eyes closed and his heart thundering. She was still so afraid.

Then Sam was there, licking his face. Brent touched the dog and his eyes opened and saw Kathy.

"I would have done better. Honestly. It wouldn't have taken me so long except for this damned nick on my forehead."

She started to laugh with relief, then she was crying again. Then she was in his arms. Jerry was smiling, too, and Brent paused to put an arm around the anxious Sam. "You're a good old dog. With good instincts. He never did like Robert," he reminded Kathy.

No, Sam had never liked Robert.

Steve searched the water until the team Jerry had called for came with masks and diving equipment. Within an hour, they found Robert. He had become entangled in the seaweed beneath the dock.

By then Kathy was sitting in a car, sipping coffee, a blanket around her. Brent told her the news, and he explained to her that the numbers had been in the main chords to the song—C, G, E. All he'd had to do was count their place in the alphabet, and he had it.

"Why Harry did that to us . . ." Brent murmured.

"Maybe he thought it was his only chance to live and see justice come to his tormenter, too."

"But he died."

"How did he know he was going to die in prison?" Kathy said. Brent, hunkered down before her, shrugged, and she knew he understood.

Keith arrived on the scene, Jerry had remembered to call him. He and Brent embraced, and Brent apologized. Keith hugged Kathy. When she whispered again that she was so sorry, he told her it was all right. He had his little son, and they were going to make it.

Steve and Jerry drove Kathy, Brent and Sam to her place. Inside, Brent shook their hands and thanked them both. "We were lucky you came. After all, you had no reason to doubt Robert. He was your lieutenant."

Steve shrugged. "Yeah, well, it was hard. He turned bad. We had to stop him. But that isn't the norm, you know, it really isn't."

Kathy smiled and pushed past Brent. She kissed Steve on the cheek. "You guys are the best. And I'll always believe in you."

Steve smiled. "He kind of soiled the badge, you know."

"He tried to," Brent corrected. "And he tried to ruin the music, too."

"Yeah, well, that's why we figured you were probably all right in there with him. He was after your wife and, in a way, all the things you believed in. I'll never think badly of musicians if you promise never to think too harshly of cops."

"It's a deal," Brent promised with a grin.

Then they were gone, and Kathy and Brent were alone. They were both crusted with seaweed and dried salt water. Suddenly Kathy started to shiver. She whispered, "It was Robert. Oh, Brent, it was Robert all the time."

"Don't think about it," he told her, sweeping her into his arms. "Don't think about it."

He carried her into the bathroom and set her down, still shivering. He started a bath and filled it with bubbles. He peeled away her clothing and set her in the water. She leaned back, and when she opened her eyes, he was with her, holding two glasses of wine.

Naked, he joined her. They drank the wine as he held her against him. She was soon drowsy, and though the pain of a friend's betrayal and death did not disappear, it was banished to a corner of her mind.

After some time he picked her up, and he laid her out on the bed. He dried her naked flesh. Then he made love to her more tenderly than he had ever done before. She slept in his arms.

In the morning, she awoke and found him fully dressed, standing by the window. He seemed to sense that her eyes were on him because he turned to her, and she could see all the anguish in his face. He walked to the bed and sat beside her.

"I was . . . I was going to leave while you were sleeping," he told her. "But then I felt I had to say goodbye."

She didn't say anything. The tears were welling in her eyes. He kissed her, a light kiss. But it became a deeper kiss, long and lingering.

"Don't go," she breathed to him.

"Kathy, I have to. If I ever hurt you again—" He tore away from her. He was on his feet and heading out the door.

She paused, her heart hammering. Then she was up, slipping on a terry robe and running after him.

He was already out the front door, heading down the walk.

"You idiot!" she called after him, and he paused, his back stiff. "You dumb idiot! Brent, I swear it, the only way for you to hurt me is to leave me! I could stand anything, anything at all, if you're with me. Don't you understand that? Brent, I love you. For the love of God, don't walk away from me again. Brent, I need you." She paused, then added softly, "Forever, my love."

She waited, and it seemed that the earth spun full around the sun, and still he stood there.

Then he turned, and he was running to her. When he reached her, he was suddenly on his knees, and he was holding her against him, his face against her belly.

Her fingers lingered over his hair. Then she held his face up to her and she whispered, "Please, don't leave me again, please."

"Do you really think we can make it?"

"I know we can."

"My temper is horrible."

"So is mine. But that's okay, Brent, don't you see? Oh, Brent you were never out of control, never,

never. It was just that with what happened, you thought...you lived with the belief— Brent, it just wasn't true! Oh, Brent..."

He was on his feet, lifting her into his arms. He stared into her eyes and said, "Kathy, I love you. Forever."

She smiled and touched his face. "Good. You can marry me again. And quickly. Okay? Enough of this living in sin. I'll even invite Marla to the wedding."

"And I'll let Axel come. Maybe we can introduce them to each other."

"Maybe," Kathy said.

He closed his eyes, then opened them. "Kathy, I'm scared."

Her eyes widened. He was never scared. She loved him for his honesty, for so many things. "I'm scared, too," she whispered. "But don't you see? It doesn't matter if we're together."

He walked with her slowly toward the house. "I hate that other place. It was always new and empty. We'll live here."

"Wonderful."

"We'll have to help Keith get back on his feet."

"Great. I'll love to take care of his baby."

"Baby! Shanna! We've got to reach her quickly."

"Soon," Kathy said, smiling. "It's just that right now, well, you know, it's not that you haven't been just wonderful already, but Brent, you're going to stay. We're engaged, right? We're going to be married. We—''

"We can go for a license right now. And head straight for a justice of the peace. The hell with the wedding. We'll invite Marla and Axel to a reception later."

Kathy smiled. "I love it. But first..."

"First?"

She grinned and whispered, "You know that awful temper of yours?"

"Mmm?"

"Well, please, ravish me, will you? Just this one last time in sin. Then we'll pick up the license and head to the justice of the peace."

"Ms. O'Hara, that's a last request I'm more than willing to fulfill," he promised her.

And proceeded to do just that.

## Epilogue

They sat in the doctor's office. Kathy's hand was in Brent's, and he was listening intently to every word Doctor Langley was saying.

"Honestly, Mr. McQueen, miscarriage is a terrible thing because people blame themselves. Women always think they did something to injure the baby. And the truth of the matter is that women lose babies because something *is* wrong. But there is absolutely no reason to fear that anything will go wrong with this pregnancy."

Brent didn't even redden, Kathy thought with amazement. His eyes were gold and intense as he leaned forward and said, "Dr. Langley, I made love to my wife very passionately and—"

"Well, Mr. McQueen, most of us wouldn't be here if that didn't happen to our parents."

"She nearly bled to death."

"The placenta pulled away. It wasn't your fault. But if it will make you feel better, abstain from sex until she's finished with her first trimester. It's never been proven that sex has anything to do with miscarriages, though. And we'll see Mrs. McQueen every two weeks. At her age, I suggest an amniocentesis."

They talked a while longer. Brent seemed relaxed, and Kathy was delighted that she had made him come.

They'd been married for seven weeks. But she must have gotten pregnant the night he broke into the house. Of course, the moment she told him, he'd panicked. He'd wanted to know why she hadn't told him before, and she'd had to explain that she hadn't known. Then she'd grinned and told him that she was awfully glad she hadn't, because she definitely didn't want to think he'd married her because he'd had to. He hadn't laughed, so she had thought that taking him to Dr. Langley would be a great idea.

"Don't you even wink at me for the next few months, young lady," Brent warned her.

She laughed and promised him, "Okay, I won't!"

She did worry that he would try to stay away from her, but he didn't. Every night they slept closely together. Tightly, tenderly.

Then came the day for the amniocentesis. She was terrified at first, but it was all right. The echo sound showed them the baby's tiny hands and feet and ribs. The nurse pointed out the four chambers of the heart, the kidneys and the brain, and she told them that the baby looked wonderful. When the doctor came, he was so pleasant and easy that he quickly had them both relaxed. He was a music lover, who teased with the nurse that they had best be good, lest Brent write them up as bad guys in a song.

Brent didn't do so very well watching the needle going into her stomach, but he was fine after that. And as the days passed after the procedure and Kathy seemed fine, he began to be more at ease.

They'd agreed to find out the sex of the baby together. The lab called to tell them that the results were normal, that the baby looked fine. Brent asked them to send a letter with the sex of the baby.

He and Kathy were going to meet for an elegant dinner. She was in her fifth month, and they were going to celebrate with a single glass of champagne, a delicious meal, and . . . sex. After they learned that of their new offspring.

When the letter came, Kathy called him at Keith's where he was working on a new album. She had a few things to do, but she'd meet him at the restaurant at eight. She'd made the reservations. She'd ordered the champagne. Everything was set.

She was stunning, he thought when he entered the restaurant and saw her. She had a glow about her. The soft silk maternity gown molded her breasts and fell softly over her growing stomach. She smiled, rose and kissed him.

"Got the letter?" he asked her.

She raised it.

"You didn't steam it open, did you?"

"Of course not!" she protested.

He signaled the waiter, who came and poured their champagne. When he disappeared, they both took a sip then smiled at each other. "Go ahead."

Kathy shoved the letter over to him. "No, you."

"All right." He slit the envelope, looking at her. "Would you rather it be a boy or a girl?"

"I don't care, you know that. What would you rather it be?"

"A healthy baby."

"We've got that."

"I guess you'd like a son."

"I don't know. Shanna is wonderful."

"Hm. Okay, so neither of us cares. Let's just open it and see."

Brent pulled out the letter and scanned it quickly. Then he began to laugh.

"Brent!" Kathy said. He was still laughing. "Brent, which sex is so damned funny?"

He shook his head. He was still laughing.

"Brent—"

"All right, all right. I see the blue fire in those eyes! Kathy, it's neither."

"What do you mean, it's neither? The baby has to be something!"

"That baby is, but Kathy, this isn't the letter. This is the bill for services rendered."

"Oh!" She snatched the letter and read it from top to bottom. Then she started to laugh, too. "Oh, Brent! The champagne, the dinner..."

"Well, they're not wasted," he said. "We'll still have them. A nice dinner and one glass of champagne for you. And I'm still on for the sex part, too," he promised blithely.

She lowered her head and smiled. "Yeah, well, I'm rather into it myself."

"Excuse me," he told her. "I'll be right back."

She toyed with her glass. It was still going to be a great night. It was just that she had been so very set to know...

Brent came back and slid into the seat. He leaned over and kissed her.

"Guess what?" he asked.

"What?"

"Blue."

"What?"

"Start buying blue." He smiled. "Kathy, it's a boy."

"How do you know?"

"I called Langley and got him out of bed. The results were sent to him right away. It's a boy, Mrs. McQueen. Very definitely a healthy little boy. And we'll keep him that way, Kath. I promise. I won't be afraid, and I won't let you be afraid."

"A boy," she murmured, grinning. She sipped her champagne and leaned against him, content.

"Brent."

"What?"

"I really think we're going to live happily ever after. I believe everything is going to be all right. And I love you so very much."

He shushed her with a long, wet kiss and then his golden eyes looked into hers.

"Forever, my love," he whispered.

She smiled and kissed him. Because she knew it was true.

\* \* \* \* \*

# Take 4 bestselling love stories FREE

## Plus get a FREE surprise gift!